W9-CVO-378

CLINT KNEW JUST HOW CLOSE
THINGS WERE GOING TO BE...

Roy Earl's arm moved, and everything was in play. It was a good clean move, a fast move, but as Clint had told Ranger First, it wasn't who was fastest, but whose shot was true...

The gunman got his gun out and almost had it straight out in front of him when Clint's first shot struck him in the chest. A surprised look came over the man's face and his arm immediately went numb—in fact, his whole body went numb and his gun fell from his hand. It struck the ground, and then he fell on top of it.

The worst day of his life, damn...

THE GUNSMITH

269

THE HANGING TREE

J. R. ROBERTS

JOVE BOOKS, NEW YORK

This is a work of fiction. Names, characters, places, and incidents either are the product of the author's imagination or are used fictitiously, and any resemblance to actual persons living or dead, business establishments, events, or locales is entirely coincidental.

THE HANGING TREE

A Jove Book / published by arrangement with
the author

PRINTING HISTORY
Jove edition / May 2004

Copyright © 2004 by Robert J. Randisi

For information address: The Berkley Publishing Group,
a division of Penguin Group (USA) Inc.
375 Hudson Street, New York, New York 10014.

ISBN: 0-515-13735-9

A JOVE BOOK®
Jove Books are published by The Berkley Publishing Group,
a division of Penguin Group (USA) Inc.,
375 Hudson Street, New York, New York 10014.
JOVE and the "J" design
are trademarks belonging to Penguin Group (USA) Inc.

PRINTED IN THE UNITED STATES OF AMERICA

10 9 8 7 6 5 4 3 2 1

ONE

"What's that look like to you, boy?" Clint asked Eclipse.

What they were looking at was a long way off, and yet it was very clear. After all, it could really have only been one thing.

"Yep," Clint said, patting the Darley Arabian's big neck, "sure looks like a man hanging from a tree to me. Now, the question is, how involved do we want to get?"

Eclipse just bobbed his head up and down a few times and pawed the ground.

"Yeah, I know," Clint said, "it's up to me."

When you spend as much time on the trail as Clint Adams did, sometimes all you can do is talk to your horse. If you talk to yourself, it would make you crazy. He had had many conversations with Duke over the years they rode together, and now he was piling them up with Eclipse.

"Well," he said, snapping the reins, "let's go and have a look, boy. There's always the possibility that the man is still alive."

A possibility, if only a slim one.

As Clint rode up to the clearing where the hanging tree was, the man's body swayed just slightly. There was just enough of a breeze to be responsible for that. He was pretty sure before he actually reached the tree that the man was dead.

He reined Eclipse in about ten feet from the tree and looked up at the dead man. He seemed young but it was hard to tell with his swollen tongue sticking out of his mouth. It was obvious that he had strangled to death rather than dying from the broken neck. Also, although his hands were tied behind his back, his feet had not been tied. He had probably kicked and danced on air for a while before he finally died. Clint wondered if the members of the lynching party who had strung him up had stayed to watch until the kicking stopped.

A quick look at the ground revealed tracks of five or six different horses. One had to be the one the hanged man had been on. There was an off chance this hanging was legal—maybe the town didn't have a scaffold built—but he doubted it. A town the size of Laredo probably would have taken the time to build one. There was a lot of rustling going on in south Texas, Clint knew. Rustlers usually grabbed some beef and then pushed them across the border where the law couldn't touch them. This was likely the work of some irate ranchers or a vigilante party.

He could have cut the man down, but then how would he have gotten him to town? Better to let the body stay where it was, where the four-legged predators couldn't get at it. There was nothing he could do about the buzzards, though. They were only now beginning to gather above the tree, which meant the man had died not very long ago. They were probably just waiting for Clint to leave.

"Sorry, fella," he said aloud. "You'll just have to hang around a little longer."

He started to turn Eclipse when a man with a rifle stepped out from behind a rock formation. He levered a round into the rifle's chamber and pointed the barrel at Clint.

"You always talk to dead men?"

"Only when my horse doesn't answer me."

The two men studied each other. The man with the rifle was young, tall, lean, but the most interesting thing about him was the Texas Ranger's badge pinned to his chest.

"You going to pull that trigger?" he asked.

"Why were you apologizing to this dead man," the ranger asked. "You string him up?"

"I had nothing to do with stringing him up," Clint said, "and I can't do anything about cutting him down, right now. I was going to ride into Laredo and get the law, let them handle it."

"Sounds like a good story," the ranger said. He lowered the rifle. "Sounds like the truth, in fact. Mind if I ask your name?"

"Clint Adams. Mind if I ask you?"

"First," the man said, "Ranger Jack First." The Ranger approached and extended his hand, which Clint shook. "Sorry about the rifle, I thought you might be one of the men responsible for this."

"You got an idea what happened here?"

"Vigilantes, most likely," First said. "This here fella's a rustler. I was sent here from Austin to catch him and bring him back."

"Well," Clint said, "looks like your job has been done for you."

"Not quite," the young ranger said. "Somebody hanged this man, and that's against the law. I need to find out who did it and bring them to justice."

"You take your badge very seriously, I see."

The man frowned. "If I wasn't going to take it seriously, why would I wear it?"

"Point taken."

"Do you mind if I ride to Laredo with you, Mr. Adams?"

"I don't mind at all, Ranger First. We can go and see the sheriff together."

"Excellent idea, sir," First said. "I'll just get my horse and we'll be on our way."

The Ranger disappeared behind the rocks and returned riding a good-looking dun. They each gave the hanging man one last look and then headed for Laredo.

TWO

The entire town of Laredo seemed ashamed.

At least, that's how it felt to Clint. As he and Ranger First rode down the main street people looked at them, and then—probably when they saw the badge on the ranger's chest—looked away. Clint wondered how many of the men had been with the vigilantes, if Ranger First's assumption was correct.

They rode to the sheriff's office and stepped down from their horses, tied them off.

"You feel it?" First asked.

"I feel it."

"I thought you might."

Together they mounted the boardwalk and approached the door to the sheriff's office. There was a shingle on the wall next to the door that read SHERIFF A. ROBY. First opened the door and entered with Clint right behind him.

"Help you gents?"

The man sat behind a desk, red-faced, about fifty or more, but sliding downhill fast. The buttons on his shirt were straining, and he either didn't have a wife to let his clothes out, or he wasn't being paid enough to buy new ones—or both.

"Sheriff Roby?" First asked.

"That's right," the man said. "Al Roby."

The ranger approached, extended his hand. Roby hesitated, then took it without rising.

"My name's First," the ranger said. "Texas Rangers."

"I can see that. Who's your friend?"

First looked at Clint and left it to him to introduce himself.

"Clint Adams." He didn't offer his hand.

"Adams?"

"That's right."

The lawman swallowed hard, then looked at First.

"He's not a ranger, is he?"

"No, he's not," First said.

"Then why's he here?"

"Because riding into town, he and I both found the same thing."

"W-what was that?"

"I think you know."

The sheriff averted his eyes, and Clint knew why. The look in Jack First's eyes—his determination to see justice done—put the older lawman to shame.

"I-I'm not sure what you mean."

"Then I'll spell it out for you. We found a man hanging from a tree outside of town, apparently the work of a group of vigilantes."

"Vigilantes?" the lawman asked. "There ain't no vigilantes in my town."

"Then he was hanged legally?" First asked. "A hanging officiated by you?"

"I didn't officiate no hanging," the lawman said. "I don't know nothin' about it."

"Well, somebody does," First said. "The man's name is Carlos Fernandez."

"The rustler?"

"That's him."

"Then what's the fuss?" Roby asked. "He got what he deserved."

"What he deserved was a trial," First said. "It was my job to come here and bring him in."

"Well, seems like somebody did your job for you," the lawman said.

First didn't reply, and Clint said, "The ranger doesn't see it that way, Sheriff."

"Well . . . whataya expect me to do?"

"First thing," the ranger said, "is to have somebody go out there, cut him down and bring him to the undertaker's."

"And then?"

"And then I expect some assistance from you in finding out who hanged him."

Again the lawman looked away. "I'll do my job."

"I hope so," First said. "I'm going to get a room at a hotel. I hope you'll let me know when the body reaches town."

"I'll send word." The sheriff looked at Clint. "Is Adams involved in this?"

"No," First said, "he just happened to ride along a bit after I did. We simply rode into town together."

"I see." Roby looked at Clint. "Will you be stayin' in town?"

"For a while," Clint said.

"What brings you this way?"

"Just passing through, Sheriff."

"Well," Roby said, "I know who you are, so I hope there won't be any trouble."

Before Clint could reply First said, "I think you have enough trouble already, Sheriff, without looking for any from Mr. Adams. How many hotels do you have in town?"

"Two," Roby said, "and several boarding houses. I don't think you'll have any trouble finding a room."

"Fine," Ranger First said. "I'll be sending a telegraph message to my captain to let him know the developments here. I'll also tell him that the local law is cooperating."

"Like I said," Roby replied. "I'll do my job."

"That's all I ask, Sheriff."

First turned and headed for the door. Clint looked at the sheriff, who tried but failed to match stares with him and finally looked away—guiltily, to Clint's way of thinking. He had the feeling that when the sheriff said he'd do his job, he meant just that—and nothing more. He was not going to go out of his way to help Ranger First with his assignment.

Clint hoped that the young ranger was as competent as he seemed to be.

THREE

"He'll be no help," Clint said when they had stepped outside.

"I'm only concerned that he not get in my way," Ranger Jack First said. "I don't like the idea of having to go against the local law."

"You might not have a choice."

First changed the subject.

"What will you do now, Mr. Adams?"

Clint shrugged. "I expected to stay in town for a day or two and rest my horse. I suppose I'll just go ahead and do that."

First looked away, studied the street intently.

"Why do you ask?"

First hesitated, then said, "My telegram to my captain. I wasn't planning on asking him to send me any help."

"And why is that?"

"Well," the Ranger said, "for one thing he told me I couldn't expect any. We're a bit shorthanded, right now."

"And for the other thing."

Ranger Jack First turned his head and looked directly at Clint Adams.

"I was figuring that maybe since you are here already and have seen what the vigilantes did, that you might consent to backing me up—if the need arose, of course."

"Of course."

"Does that mean yes?"

Clint sighed and said, "That means we need to discuss it over a beer—and you're buying."

They repaired to the nearest saloon. Little Nicky's Saloon was a small place which, at midday, was not doing very much business. Ranger First bought two beers from a bored looking bartender and carried them to the back table Clint had already laid claim to.

"Thanks, Jack," Clint said. "I can call you Jack, can't I? Instead of Ranger First?"

"If you like."

"And you can call me Clint."

"Fine."

Clint sipped his beer and set the mug down. First's beer remained on the table in front of him, untouched.

"What kind of help do you want, Jack?" Clint asked.

"Just back up if I need it," First said.

"What are you going to try to do?"

"Find out who the vigilantes were who hanged Fernandez," the Ranger said. " Find out who their leader was. Bring them all to justice."

"That's all?"

"For starters," First said. "If I find out the sheriff had anything to do with it, I'll arrest him, too, and have him replaced."

"What's your first step going to be?"

First sat back.

"I figure the ranchers around here were tired of having their cows rustled," he said. "They're the ones with the biggest motive to kill Fernandez. I'll start asking questions there."

"Ranch hands?"

"Hands, foremen, the owners," Frist said.

"You've got some of the biggest ranchers in Texas in the area, Jack," Clint said. "You just going to ride up to their homes and ask them if they're vigilantes?"

First sat forward in his seat, placed his hand around the handle of his beer mug. Clint wondered if the young man was actually going to take a sip.

"Sometimes the direct route is the best," Jack First said and lifted the mug to his lips.

"Look," Clint said, "maybe I can stick around until you finish your investigation—and maybe I should go with you when you question the ranchers . . ."

"You have no authority," First said, "and I don't have the authority to make you a ranger, or a deputy."

"I don't want to be either," Clint said. "I just want to keep you from getting killed. I don't think I need much authority to do that, do I?"

First frowned, as if the question—or the answer—vexed him, and said, "I guess not."

"Then the first thing we better do is get some rooms and get settled," Clint said. "My horse could use a rubdown, some feed and some rest."

"Rest?" First said. "I wanted to get started right away—"

"You have to check into a hotel and send your telegram," Clint said. "You also have to get something to eat." He stood up. "I think your investigation can start first thing in the morning, don't you?"

"But—"

"Come on," Clint said. "Let's get settled and I'll buy you a steak dinner."

"I have money."

"Not much, I'm sure," Clint said. "I know the Rangers don't pay much, and you have to buy all your own equipment and supplies. Let me do my part and buy you that steak."

"Well," First said, "I am kind of hungry."

"Good," Clint said. "Livery stable first and then a hotel."

First took a second minute sip of his beer, set it down and followed Clint out of the saloon.

FOUR

After they had put their horses up at the livery stable, Clint wanted to stay in a hotel while Ranger First preferred a rooming house.

"Better beds and meals," First said, but Clint thought it might have had something to with the Ranger having to pay his own way.

"You get yourself situated," Clint said, "and then we'll meet back at that same saloon at about . . . what . . . seven?"

"Seven's good," First said. "I'll see you then."

They split up in front of the livery, each going off in search of their own lodging.

Sheriff Roby watched as Clint and Jack First went into the livery with their horses and came out without them. When they went their separate ways he was confused as to which one to follow. But since he was more afraid of Clint Adams than the ranger, he followed Jack First.

First found a rooming house at the north end of town by asking directions from two women who looked like church-going ladies.

"Would you ladies be able to direct me to a decent rooming house?" he asked them.

Both women stopped and stared at him suspiciously for a moment, but then noticed his badge and relaxed a bit.

"You're not looking for a house of ill repute, are you, young man?" one of them asked.

"No, ma'am," First said, holding his hat in his hand. "I need a place where I can get a good night's sleep and a decent meal to start the day. I've got a job to do hereabouts and I don't think I'll have time for any of . . . that."

The women regarded him with satisfaction now and gave him directions.

"The Widow Connolly has a very nice house at the north end of town, young man," the second woman said. "You tell her Henrietta Willoughby sent you over and she'll see you get a comfy bed."

"And she'll feed you till you're bursting," the first woman said.

"I'm much obliged to you both, ladies," First said, replacing his hat on his head.

As he headed off in the direction they indicated he heard one say to the other, "What a nice young man."

The sheriff watched Jack First go up to the Widow Connolly's door and enter, and then not come back out for some time. Satisfied that this was where the ranger would be staying, he turned and walked back to the center of town to his office, where he found his deputy, Stan Kellogg, all wet-behind-the-ears twenty-two years of him.

"Where the hell have you been?" he demanded.

Kellogg, who had been sitting in the sheriff's chair, jumped up and started to stammer.

"Never mind," Sheriff Roby said. "Just make sure you're around here if anything happens for the next few hours. I have to leave town for a while."

"Where you goin', sheriff?"

"I have to see Mr. Waxman."

Kellogg looked impressed as Roby invoked the name of the biggest rancher in the county.

"Somethin' up?" the deputy asked.

"Yes, something is up," the sheriff said. "We've got a Texas Ranger in town, as well as Clint Adams."

Kellogg swallowed hard. "You mean . . . the Gunsmith?"

"Yes, that Clint Adams."

"Well, what are they doin' here?"

"Whataya think?"

Kellogg frowned a moment, then asked, "The hangin'?"

"Very good, Stan."

"What does the Gunsmith care about a hanged cattle rustler?" the young man asked.

"I don't know," Roby said, "but he rode in with the ranger, so he must be interested somehow."

"You talked to them?"

"Yeah, I did."

"Both of them?"

"That's right."

"W-what's he like?"

"The ranger?" the Sheriff asked. "He's sort of wet-behind-the-ears like you."

"No, I meant the Gunsmith," Kellogg said, eagerly. "What's he like, Sheriff?"

Not wanting the deputy to know he was impressed with—or afraid of—the Gunsmith, Roby said, "He was like a man, Stan. He was just like any man."

Kellogg looked disappointed.

"Just stay around here, okay?" Roby said. "Don't get lost. I'll be back tonight."

"Yes, sir," Kellogg said. "I'll be on the job."

As the sheriff went out the door, Kellogg turned and reached for the gun rack on the wall. Suddenly, the door opened again and the sheriff shouted, "And stay away from the shotguns!"

FIVE

Frank Waxman listened patiently while Sheriff Al Roby told him about the ranger, Jack First and Clint Adams. They were in his office in his house and his foreman, Ben Pearson, was standing in the corner also listening. He had shown the lawman into Waxman's office and his boss had told him to remain in the room.

"So the ranger is going to look for the killers of his cattle thief?" Waxman asked.

"That's what he said."

Waxman looked at Pearson, who said, "They oughtta find out who did it and pin a medal on him."

"And what about Adams?" Waxman asked. "Is he going to be helping the ranger with his investigation?"

"He says he's just passing through, Mr. Waxman."

"I can send him on his way, boss," Pearson said, confidently.

"Who are you kidding, Ben?" Waxman said. "He'd kill you in a minute."

"Boss—"

He broke off as at that moment Leslie Waxman, his boss's wife, entered. She was blond and beautiful and, at forty, about twenty years younger than her rancher husband.

17

"Oh, I'm sorry," she said, stopping short. "I didn't know you were busy."

"Just doing some business, dear," Waxman said. "Did you want something?"

"I just wanted to talk to you about our dinner party," she said. "It's not important. It can wait."

"I won't be very long," he said. "I'll come and find you when we're done here."

"All right, dear." She turned, said, "Hello, Ben," and walked out. Sheriff Roby thought he caught something between the two, but Waxman's attention was elsewhere.

Pearson looked over at the lawman and smirked.

"Sheriff," Waxman said, "is the ranger going to send for help?"

"I don't think so," Roby said. "He did say something about sending a telegram to his captain, but I think he was just going to be checking in, not asking for help."

"All right," Waxman said, "so we'll have one young ranger wandering around asking questions. If the vigilantes hear about it, he's going to be in a lot of trouble."

"Unless he does get help from Adams," Roby pointed out.

"Like I said, boss—"

"No, Ben," Waxman said, "I want you to stay away from Clint Adams. That's a direct order. Do you understand?"

"Sure, boss."

"Roby," Waxman said, "go back to town and keep an eye on the ranger."

"What do I do if he does get in trouble?"

Waxman gave Roby a hard stare and said, "Just do your job, Sheriff. That's all you have to do."

"Yes, sir."

"Just don't go looking for trouble," Waxman said. "Do you know what I mean?"

The lawman wasn't sure he did but he said, "Yes, sir, I, uh, understand."

"Good," Waxman said. "Keep me informed."

"I will."

"Show yourself out, Sheriff," Waxman said. "I have to talk to Ben, here."

As the lawman started out the door Waxman said, "Roby."

"Yes, sir."

"Why did you bring this information to me?" the rancher asked. "Do you think I had anything to do with the hanging?"

"Oh, uh, no, sir, I just thought you should, uh, know, uh, because you're . . . uh, well, you know."

"Yeah," Ben Pearson said, "we know, Sheriff."

"You can go," Waxman said.

"Yes, sir."

Waxman gave the lawman time to walk down the hall and out of the house, then said to Pearson, "Close the door, Ben. I don't want Leslie walking in on us again."

Pearson closed the door. When he turned and saw his boss had seated himself behind his desk, he walked over and sat in a chair across from him.

"Warning me off Adams, boss," he asked, "was that for Roby's benefit?"

"No, I meant it," Waxman said. "I don't want you to go near Adams. Besides, why should we mess with him if he's just passing through?"

"What about the ranger?"

"What about him?" the older man asked. "I didn't have anything to do with any vigilante hanging, did you?"

"No, sir."

"Then why should we worry about him?"

"Well . . . he'll be pokin' around."

"Let him," Waxman said. "He's not going to find anything . . . but just to be on the safe side, pick out a man you trust and have him watch Adams."

"Yes, sir." He got up and started for the door.

"And Ben."

"Yes, sir?"

"Make it someone who knows how to use a gun," Waxman said, "just in case."

SIX

Clint got himself a room at the Laredo House Hotel, and asked the desk clerk for a good place to get a steak.

"You could get one right here in the dining room, sir," the man said, pointing.

"I want a very good steak, though."

"Well, in that case," the young man said, "I'd recommend the First Street Café. It's just down the street—"

"On First Street," Clint finished.

"Yes, sir."

"Thanks."

He left the hotel and walked down the street, having to pass the café on his way to Little Nicky's Saloon. He peered in the window and saw that it was a small place with eight or ten tables, only a few of which were taken. He hoped that was still the case when he returned with Ranger First. He was suddenly ravenous. He'd opted to have only coffee that morning before breaking camp. Consequently, he had not eaten since the night before.

Jack First came down from his room and encountered his new landlady, the Widow Connolly. He was still surprised to find that she was so young and pretty. Older than him by a few years but still very young . . .

"Having your husband die has nothing to do with age," she'd told him when they met.

"I'm sorry," he said, realizing he'd been staring. "When they told me you were the *Widow* Connolly I thought—"

"Most people do," she said, cutting him off.

They made arrangements for him to have a room, and she gave him a discount because he was an "officer of the law."

"I can pay," he'd assured her.

"I'm sure you can," she'd said, "but I think we need to help our peacekeepers as much as we can. It's our duty as citizens of this country."

At that moment, Ranger Jack First thought he might be in love . . .

"Where are you off to, Ranger First?" she asked. "Dinner is almost ready."

"I'm sorry, Mrs. Connolly, but I have a previous engagement for dinner. My first meal with you and your other boarders will have to be breakfast, I'm afraid."

Her pretty face betrayed her disappointment, but she recovered very quickly.

"Very well," she said, "that's your choice. Will you be coming back in late this evening?"

"I don't think so, ma'am," he said. "I should be back early."

"Fine," she said. "Please be as quiet as you can when you return. I have two boarders who turn in quite early."

"Yes, ma'am," he said, "I'll keep that in mind."

"Have a pleasant evening, Ranger First." She turned and walked across the living room to the kitchen. He watched her trim figure until she disappeared into the kitchen, then scolded himself and reminded himself to keep his mind on business.

He left the boarding house and headed for his meeting with Clint Adams.

Clint was seated with a beer in front of him when the Ranger entered Little Nicky's. The saloon was now busier than it had been when they were there earlier, about two-thirds full, and all eyes were on the young ranger as he crossed the room and sat at the table with Clint.

"A beer?" Clint asked.

"Not right now."

"Did you get yourself situated?"

"I did, yes," the other man said. "And you?"

"Got a room at the Laredo House."

"I'm at a boarding house at the north end of town, run by the Widow Connolly."

"Ah," Clint said, "short, fat and fifty?"

"Actually," First said, "tall, slender, about thirty and very pretty."

"Doesn't sound like any landlady I ever had at a rooming house."

"She's heard all of that before."

"Well, are you hungry?"

First frowned. "I hadn't thought about it, but I am, yes."

Clint drained half the beer and left the other half in the mug on the table.

"Let's go, then," he said, standing up. "I found a place that's supposed to have a good steak."

First stood and they walked together to the batwing doors and exited the saloon.

"You seem to be getting lots of attention," Clint said, once they were outside.

"Any of those men in the saloon could be vigilantes," First said. "I admit to feeling an itch in the middle of my back."

"I guess you need someone to watch that back for you," Clint said.

"Maybe we can talk about that over dinner," the Ranger said.

Clint pointed the way and they walked to the café to check out the steaks.

SEVEN

"Did you see him?" Clint asked as they entered the café.

"Doorway, right across the street from the saloon?" the ranger asked.

Clint was impressed. It was still up in the air as to how good the ranger would be at his job. The fact that he'd seen the man who'd been watching them was a good sign.

"Gentlemen?"

They turned and saw a blond waitress in her thirties smiling at them with her pretty mouth and her amazing blue eyes.

"A table?"

"Please," Clint said. "Someone told me we could find a good steak here."

She laughed and said, "You can find more than one good steak here. I think I can arrange for at least two."

"Sounds good," Clint said, "but we'll need a table in a corner, away from the window."

At that moment the woman seemed to notice Rangers First's badge.

"I see," she said. "That shouldn't be a problem. We have plenty of tables."

Actually, five of the ten tables were empty, and there happened to be one in a corner. She led them to it and they seated themselves in a way that could afford them both a view of the door.

"Two steak dinners?" she asked.

"That's what we're here for," Clint said. "And maybe we could start with some coffee?"

"Comin' up," she said. "My name's Angela."

"Hello, Angela," Clint said. "I'm Clint, and this is Jack."

"Ranger Jack?" she asked, giving the young ranger a smile.

"Actually, it's Ranger First," he said.

"Well Ranger First and Clint," she said, "I'll be right back with your coffee."

"Very pretty girl," Clint said.

"I suppose," First said, thinking she wasn't as pretty as his widowed landlady.

"Let's talk a bit about watching each other's back," Clint said.

"Why would you need your back watched?" First asked. "I'm the one with the badge."

"Well, for one thing I always need my back watched," Clint answered. "That's just the nature of who I am."

"I can understand that."

"But now we've got somebody watching either you or me," Clint said. "We don't know which."

"Me."

"Why?"

First patted his badge. "I'm the one who's going to cause trouble."

"But for who?" Clint asked. "That's the question. Who's having you watched?"

"Obviously," First said, "the sheriff must have told some-one about me—someone he works for."

"Might make sense to ask him, then," Clint said.

"Maybe not."

"Why?"

They suspended the conversation when Angela came over

with a pot of coffee and two cups. Clint noticed that they were the center of attention for the other diners in the place.

"I'll bet you're here about the hanging," she said to First, as she poured his cup full.

"Does everyone know about that?" he asked.

"Pretty much," she said.

"Does everyone know who did it?" Clint asked.

"Now that I can't say," she replied. "Most folks figure it was the work of vigilantes, but since the hanged man was a rustler, nobody really cares much who did it."

"I care," First said.

"Well, that's your job, isn't it?"

"That's right."

"And you?" she asked, looking at Clint. "Why are you here in Laredo?"

"Well," Clint said, "right now it's to have a steak dinner."

"Right," she said, "right, I'll get that for you."

As she walked away Jack First said, "She has lots of questions for a waitress."

"Maybe she has some answers, too," Clint said. "I guess I could work on that a bit. What will be your first move in the morning?"

"I thought I'd ride out and talk to all the ranchers in the area," First said. "They all certainly had a stake in seeing Fernandez dead."

"Makes sense. Plan on going alone?"

"I did," First said. "You got other ideas?"

Clint sighed.

"Ranger, I think that by riding into town and going to see the sheriff with you I sort of caused us to be joined at the hip for a while," Clint said. "I don't think I have any choice but to ride along with you. Might keep both of us alive a while longer, that way."

"Well, Clint," First said, "I'm not going to turn down that offer, but you do have another option."

"And what's that?"

"You could mount up tomorrow, ride out of town and just keep going."

"I suppose I could," Clint said, after a moment, "but somehow, it just isn't in me."

EIGHT

The steaks turned out to be excellent. They were cooked—
and served—to perfection, and when she brought their check
over Clint told Angela so.

"Thank you kindly," she said. "We pride ourselves on
good food and good service."

"Is the cook your husband?" Clint asked.

"Heavens, no," she said. "I just work here. Art is the
owner and the cook, and he's a little too old and a lot too
fat for me to marry."

"So then there is no husband?" Clint asked.

Angela looked away shyly and said, "Not at the moment,
no."

"How are you at serving breakfast?"

"What?"

"I mean here," Clint said, "tomorrow morning."

"Oh," she said, "yes, well, we do a brisk breakfast business from about seven to nine."

"Maybe I could reserve a seat now?" Clint asked. "For
say, 8 A.M.?"

She smiled and said, "I'll see what I can do."

"Or should I make it two?" Clint asked First.

"No," the ranger said, "that's all right. I have other plans."

"Well, then," Clint said to Angela, "I guess it'll just be me. I'll see you at eight, then."

"Have a nice evening, gentlemen," she said.

They stepped outside, stepped away from the doorway and stopped. Neither of them looked directly across the street, but they both knew the man was there, in one of the doorways.

"How about that beer now?" Clint asked.

"Sounds good," First said, "but I'll buy."

"The first one," Clint said, "you can buy the first one."

Clarence Stratton followed Clint Adams and the ranger from the café back to Little Nicky's Saloon. The place was lit up, now, and in full swing, with music and loud voices coming from inside. Stratton was about to cross the street and follow them in when he saw three horses hitched up outside the place and recognized them as coming from Mr. Waxman's WX spread. He turned, found himself a comfortable doorway and settled in to wait.

Something was bound to happen sooner or later.

Actually, there were more than three WX men in town that night. Three of them were in the saloon, but the fourth—Ben Pearson—was over at Molly's Cathouse, two blocks away. One of Molly's best girls was at work between his legs, busily sucking on him until he was about ready to explode.

"Hey, girl!" he said, pushing her off him. "Not so damned fast. I got time to spend."

"And money?" she asked.

"Don't I always?"

Lily Thomas sat back on her haunches and eyed the WX foreman. She was dark-haired and full-breasted and very, very talented. There had been a time when Pearson visited her three or four times a week, but lately it had tapered off to once a week, or even longer.

"You don't come around as much as you used to, Ben," she complained, with a pout.

"I've been busy, Lil." His vest was hanging on the bedpost. He reached into a pocket for the makings and started rolling himself a cigarette.

"Or maybe you're gettin' satisfied somewhere else?" she asked. "By somebody else?"

"What are you talkin' about?"

"It happens all the time, Ben," she said. She sat back, leaning on her hands; the movement caused her breasts to swell and separate a bit. Her brown nipples were distended, the largest he'd ever seen on a woman, which had always been part of the fascination for him. "We get lots of husbands in here who ain't gettin' it at home, only once in a while their wives get randy—certain time of the year, I guess—and start satisfyin' them a little more. They stop comin' around as often, but it soon wears off and they come back regular, like."

Pearson struck a lucifer, lit his cigarette and shook the match to death.

"I ain't married," he said.

"That don't mean you ain't got a woman somewhere," she said, "maybe hidden away?"

"You don't know what you're talkin' about, Lil."

"Maybe not," she said, but she wasn't convinced.

Pearson stood up and walked naked to the window. He opened it, and was able to hear the voices and music from Little Nicky's. He knew some of his boys were there, and he knew they were on the lookout for the ranger and for Clint Adams. Leaving the window open would assure him of hearing if anything started to happen over there.

He tossed the lit cigarette out the window and turned to look at the busty whore.

"Let's finish what we started, girl," he said. "Might be some excitement outside tonight, and I don't wanna miss it."

"Oh," she said, "*now* you're in a hurry . . ."

NINE

When Clint walked into the saloon with Jack First he could feel the tension in the air. Whoever the vigilantes were, some of them had to be in that room. If those men suddenly pulled guns, they'd probably be in a lot of trouble—and it would only take one of them to get it started. However, vigilantes operated as a group and a cowardly group, at that. They needed a leader to follow, and if there wasn't one in the room, they'd do nothing.

There were no tables available so Clint and First went to the bar and ordered a beer each. Nervously, the bartender set the mugs in front of them. Clint wondered if he was usually nervous, or if there was something in particular that was making his hands shake.

"You okay, friend?" he asked.

"Huh? Who me?" the fortyish, squatly built man asked. He seemed surprised that Clint had spoken to him.

"Your hands are shaking," First said.

Abruptly, the bartender pushed his hands behind his back.

"I, uh, don't know w-what you're talkin' about. 'scuse me," the man stammered. "I gotta go."

They watched as he almost ran to the other end of the bar.

"Something's scaring the hell out of him," Clint observed.

"Might be you," Jack First said.

Clint looked at him.

"Unfortunately, you might be right."

They sipped the beer and used the mirror behind the bar to look the room over.

"I wonder who Little Nicky is?" Clint asked.

As if on cue a short man—barely five-six—approached them and said, "Gentlemen."

They both turned to face him. He looked to be in his thirties, clean shaven and confident, as if he didn't even realize he was the shortest man in the room. He wore an expensive black suit, a shirt and tie and a pie pin that looked like a real pearl. He belonged in Portsmouth Square in San Francisco, not a saloon in Laredo.

"Welcome," he said. "Allow me to introduce myself. I'm Nicolas Taylor."

"Little Nicky?" Clint asked, before he even realized what he was saying.

"That's right," the man replied, unoffended. But then why would he be offended, if he named his own place? He stuck out his hand. "And you're Clint Adams."

"That's right."

Clint shook the man's hand and found his grip impressive—possibly deliberately so. Maybe Nicolas Taylor wasn't as comfortable with his size as he seemed.

"You're a very famous man," Taylor said, after the handshake. "I'm honored to have you in my place."

"We're just having a beer," Clint said.

"On me, by the way," Little Nicky said. "I'll take care of it. And your friend's name?"

"First," the ranger replied, "Ranger Jack First."

The two men shook hands. Clint thought that First was probably only a few years younger than Nicolas Taylor.

"I prefer to be called Nick," Taylor said.

"Well, Nick," Clint said, "if you don't mind me asking,

how did you end up running a place in Laredo? You seem more suited for San Francisco?"

"Do I?" Taylor looked pleased. "I'll take that as a compliment."

"It's how I meant it."

"Let's just say I ended up here," Taylor said. "I was passing through, got into a poker game and the next thing I knew I owned this place."

Clint knew lots of men—gamblers—who became businessmen that way. Many things ended up on the table and in the pot of high-stakes poker games.

"How long ago was that?" Clint asked.

"About four years."

"Do you like Laredo?" Clint asked.

Nick Taylor shrugged.

"It's a town, like a lot of towns."

"Not quite like a lot of towns," Jack First said.

"How do you mean?" Taylor asked.

"A lot of towns don't have vigilante hangings."

Taylor frowned, then said, "Oh, you mean that rustler who got hanged outside of town? Is that who did it, vigilantes?"

"Isn't it?" the ranger asked.

"Well, I don't know," Taylor said. "I guess I just assumed he got somebody mad at him."

"Somebody like a local rancher?" First asked.

"Or some of his own men?" Taylor asked. "Maybe he cheated them and they didn't like it?"

"That's a possibility, I guess," First said.

"But you're going to operate under the assumption of vigilantes, aren't you?"

"Yes."

"Your choice, I suppose," the little gambler said. "You're the expert. You know better than I do. Gentlemen, please, enjoy your stay at Little Nicky's. There's food, drink, gambling and fine women."

"Nick," Clint said as the man started to turn away.

"Yes, Clint?"

"Why did you come over here?"

The man smiled. "You're strangers in town. I just wanted to welcome you to my place."

"That's all?"

"That's all," Taylor said, then added, "for now," and walked away.

TEN

"What do you suppose that was about?" Jack First asked.

"Maybe just what he said," Clint replied. "Welcoming us to his place."

"Or maybe feeling us out."

"You think he might be the vigilante leader?" Clint asked.

"Why? You don't?"

"Not out front, anyway," Clint said.

"What do you mean?"

"It'd be kind of hard for him to ride with a bunch of vigilantes—and especially to lead them—and not have his size be noticed."

"So you think he might be leading behind the scenes?"

"If he's involved at all," Clint said. "That'd be my bet."

"Then we'd still need to find out who actually leads them," First said. "A bunch of vigilantes need a leader who can fire them up and actually ride with them. They're too cowardly to do it, otherwise."

Clint turned his head and looked at the young ranger.

"You sound like you've had experiences with vigilantes before."

Grimly, Jack First said, "You could say that. I've seen them in action, firsthand."

When he didn't elaborate, Clint decided not to push. The
two men stood in silence, finishing their beers. Clint had the
feeling that since Nick Taylor had come over and talked to
them the tension level had gone up even more, in the room.
The smart thing to do might be to finish their beers and either
retire for the night, or find someplace less crowded to drink.

The decision, however, came too late.

Across the room from them was a table of three men, all
cowhands from the WX spread. As Nick Taylor walked by
their table he gave a barely perceptible nod to one of them,
who returned it.

"That them?" Gaylord Horn asked.

"Dummy," Tony Dundee said from across the table.
"Nicky said he'd go up to them and talk to them to point
them out to us. Ain't that what he done?"

"You're both stupid," the third hand, Marty Roby, said.
"Don't you see the badge on the Texas Ranger? What more
did you need?"

"Just because your brother's the sheriff you notice badges,
Marty," Dundee said.

"Yeah," Horn said, "how's your brother gonna feel about
you pickin' a fight with a Texas Ranger?"

"What's he gonna care?" Roby asked. "He's gettin' paid
just like everybody else, ain't he?"

"You boys want somethin' else?"

They'd been so busy talking that they hadn't noticed Annie Parker come sidling up to their table.

"I want somethin' else, Annie," Tony Dundee said to her,
winking.

"I mean somethin' that won't make me sick to my stomach," the busty little redhead said.

Horn started to cackle with glee and the girl rolled her
eyes and looked at Marty Roby.

"We don't need any more drinks, Annie," he said.
"Thanks."

She nodded and headed across the room to the bar.

"When do we do this?" Horn asked.

"Before they leave the saloon, stupid," Roby said.

"This is gonna be fun," Dundee said, still stinging from Annie's rejection and wanting to take it out on someone. "I ain't broke anybody's bones in weeks."

Roby looked at the larger of the three men and said, "Well, you'll get your chance, Tony. Yes, sir, you'll get your chance."

"Who's the other fella?" Horn asked.

"I don't know," Roby said. "Nobody told me that."

"He don't look like he'll be any trouble at all," Big Tony Dundee said.

Annie went up to the bar and stood next to Clint, without looking at him. Clint noticed her because she was young, pretty, had red hair and pale skin, and vitality radiated from her.

"Hey, mister," she said, to him, then hurriedly added, "no, don't look at me."

"You want me to talk to you without looking at you?" Clint asked. "How about if I use the mirror?"

"That's fine," she said. "See that table of three men I was just standin' at?"

"I'm sorry," he said, hating to admit it, "but I didn't see what table you were—"

"The one with the three ranch hands—one of them bigger than a grizzly and with more hair."

Clint turned and surveyed the room, spotted the big man she was talking about and turned back around, doing it all nonchalantly.

"Now I see them."

"Well, they're gonna start some trouble for you and your friend, so you better get out of here while you can."

"Trouble for us?"

"More for your friend the ranger than you, but yeah."

"What ranch are they from?"

"They work at the WX, biggest spread around here."

"Well, thanks for the warning."

"Just don't want to see two handsome men gettin' their bones broke by stupid Tony Dundee, that's all."

"What's your name?"

"Annie?"

"I owe you, Annie."

Now Annie looked at him, smiled and said, "I'll collect."

As she moved away from the bar, Clint nudged Jack First and passed on the warning.

"You want to get out of here?" Clint asked.

"This might be more than just some ranch hands wanting to have fun, Clint," First said. "Maybe this has something to do with why I'm here."

"So you don't want to leave?"

First looked at Clint, who thought that this would be a good test for the two of them, to see how well they worked together. It would also give him a chance to judge whether or not the young ranger was competent enough to watch his back.

"Why don't we stick around and see what develops?" First suggested.

"Okay," Clint said. "You're the man with the badge. I'll let you decide whether we get into trouble or not."

"Just this once," Jack First said, "let's."

ELEVEN

The three WX men stood up, hitched up their gunbelts and walked to the bar.

"Ain't no room for us at the bar, Marty," Gaylord Horn said.

"Ah, these two gents'll let us have their spots, won't you, fellas?" Roby asked Clint and First.

Jack First gave Marty Roby a brief over-the-shoulder look, then turned his back and said, "There's room at the other end of the bar."

"Yeah," Roby said, "but my friends and me, we like this end of the bar."

"You had a table," Clint said, without looking at them. "Why don't you go back to it?"

"We don't wanna sit at a table anymore," Roby said. "We wanna stand at the bar."

"Other end," Jack First said.

"My friend, here, he's got his heart set on this end of the bar," Roby said. "Don't you, Tony?"

"Yeah," Dundee said, stepping forward. He put his left hand on Jack First's shoulder and his right hand on Clint's shoulder. They each felt as if a bear had laid its paw on them. "I want this end of the bar. I can see the girls better."

41

Clint looked at the big man and said, "Friend, you don't want to stand here."

"I don't?" Dundee asked, with a frown. "Why not?"

"Because then all the girls will be able to see you."

"What's wrong with that?"

"Nothing," Clint said, "if you like nightmares."

"What's that supposed to mean?" Dundee asked, his confusion deepening.

"Are you stupid?' Jack First asked, turning his head to look up at the man. "He's saying that seeing you will give the girls nightmares."

Dundee blinked at First.

"Because you're ugly," the ranger added.

"And big," Clint added.

"And ugly," First said again.

"Hey," Dundee said, finally understanding, "are you making fun of me?"

"Now he gets it," Clint said to First.

"Took him long enough."

Roby and Horn stared at each other, wondering why these two crazy men were trying to get Big Tony Dundee mad.

"Hey!" Dundee roared. He tightened his hold on their shoulders and yanked them around.

Both men were ready, and as they pivoted around to face the big man they both swung their beer mugs and smashed them over the big man's head.

If the thick glass breaking over his head hurt him at all maybe the cold beer cascading down over him revived him. Instead of keeling over like they expected, the big man released Clint's shoulder, grabbed ahold of Jack First with both hands and—before Clint could react—lifted the younger man up over his head and tossed him over the bar. First crashed into the mirror, smashing it, and also smashing a bunch of bottles on his way down. He fell behind the bar and out of sight.

Dundee then turned on Clint, whose hand flew to his gun

and palmed it. He would have fired but he suddenly realized that the big man was not wearing a gunbelt.

"You can't shoot him," Roby said. "He doesn't wear a gun."

"He don't like them," Gaylord Horn said.

"So if you shoot him, you'd be shooting an unarmed man in front of all these people."

Dundee stood there, glaring at Clint as beer and some rivulets of blood made their way over his face to his chin, where they joined and dripped off.

"Let's call an end to this then," Clint suggested.

"Can't," Roby said. "You got him mad. When Dundee gets mad he's got to break something."

"Like an arm or a leg," Horn said.

"Or a head," Roby said.

"Well," Clint said, holstering his gun, "maybe he did that already. Maybe he broke my friend for good. How about letting me check on him?"

Roby put his hand on Dundee's chest as the big man took a step forward.

"Let him check on his ranger friend, Tony," Roby said. "For all the good it'll do him." To Clint he said, "I seen Dundee here take apart six men at one time. So you go ahead and see if your friend is awake and in one piece."

"Much obliged," Clint said.

He climbed over the bar, keeping a wary eye on the big man and peered over the side. Jack First was lying on his back, staring up at the ceiling, his eyes not quite focused.

"You all right?" he asked.

"I think so."

"Anything broken?"

"N-no."

"Then you want to get out here and give me a hand?"

TWELVE

Clint reached down to give First a hand. When the ranger had struggled to his feet, he assisted him in climbing back over the bar. He had lost his hat, and there was some glass in his hair.

They both turned to face Tony Dundee and his two partners. The others in the room had backed away, lining the walls and watching the action near the bar. The bartender had vanished.

"I'm gonna break you both in half," Dundee said.

"Do it, Tony," Marty Roby said, and both he and Gaylord Horn backed away to give their friend room.

"What do you think?" Clint asked.

First, still hurting from being hurled over the bar, said, "I think we should shoot him."

"He's unarmed."

"So what?" First said. "He's got hands, and he's going to use them to hurt us."

"Have you ever shot an unarmed man?" Clint asked.

"Not yet. You?"

Clint frowned, then shook his head and said, "You know, I can't remember."

"Stop talking," Dundee said, "and fight." He took off the

45

black hat he wore and tossed it away, then rolled up his sleeves.

"Legs," Clint said.

"Right," First said.

They each drew their guns and shot the big man in a leg. It was probably lucky for him they hadn't picked the same leg. The big man grunted, staggered, but did not go down.

"Hey!" Marty Roby yelled.

Clint and First both holstered their guns.

"It's over, boy," Jack First said. "Get your friend to a doctor."

But Tony Dundee wasn't done. He took two halting steps towards them, then a third before he stopped and succumbed to the pain in his legs.

"Y-you shot me!" he said, stunned.

"Yes," Clint said. "Sorry."

"You didn't leave us much choice," First said.

"This ain't over," Roby said.

"I don't have time to arrest you boys," First said. "I suggest you take your friend to the doctor."

"Before the sheriff gets here," Clint added.

Marty Robby laughed. "The sheriff is my brother. He's not gonna arrest me."

"Well, we're not, either," Clint said. "You know what that means."

"What?" Horn asked.

"If you don't take your friend and leave," Clint said, "and if you go for yours guns, we'll have to kill you."

Clint looked at Dundee, whose trousers were becoming soaked with his blood. "Come on, boys," he said. "Get him to a doctor before he bleeds to death."

"I'd listen to Mr. Adams, if I was you," First said.

"Adams?" Roby said.

"Yes," Jack First said. "Clint Adams."

Roby and Horn both gaped at Clint.

"He's Clint Adams?" Roby asked.

"Yes," the Ranger said.

"The Gunsmith?" Horn asked.

"Yes."

"Jesus Christ!" Horn said, backhanding Roby in his chest. "You expect me to slap leather with the Gunsmith?"

"I-I didn't know . . ." Roby said.

"Marty," Dundee said, "it hurts."

"Yeah," Roby said, "yeah, okay, Tony. We'll get you to the doc."

Roby got on one side of the big man, Horn the other, and they walked him out of the saloon.

Clint and First exchanged a glance, and each heaved a sigh of relief. The other men in the saloon began reclaiming their tables and chairs.

"Where's that bartender?" Clint asked. "I need a drink."

"Whiskey, this time," First said. "Whiskey."

THIRTEEN

Clint was about to go behind the bar himself when Annie appeared and saved him the trouble.

"You boys deserve this," she said, pouring them each a shot.

"I'd like a beer to follow this up," Clint said. "Whiskey's not usually my drink, but this seems like a special occasion."

He and First clinked glasses and downed the whiskey.

"You sure you're all right?" Clint asked.

"A little sore," First said, "but I'll live."

"That was great!" Annie said. "I was wondering how you were going to stop Dundee from breaking you in two—or four."

Clint looked around the place. For the most part men had returned to what they were doing before the excitement. Only a few had taken the opportunity to leave. There were two other women working the room, and they didn't seem to mind the excitement.

"Did a little damage behind the bar," Jack First said. "Where's Mr. Taylor? I'd like to apologize."

"He disappeared when the fight started," Annie said.

"So did the bartender," Clint pointed out. "Maybe one of them went for the sheriff."

"Hmph," Annie said, placing a mug of beer in front of each of them. "Fat lot of good he would do."

"Then that fella wasn't lying?" Clint asked. "He really is the sheriff's brother?"

"Yup," she said. "Marty Roby."

"I guess it's a good thing we didn't have to kill him," Clint said to the ranger.

First nodded, stretched his neck, arched his back and then drank some beer.

"Maybe you should get back to your boarding house and get some rest," Clint said.

"If past experience is any indication," First said. "I'm going to feel a lot worse in the morning. I'd like to put that off for as long as possible."

"Amen to that," Clint said, and they clinked glasses. At that moment the batwing doors opened and the sheriff walked in with the bartender behind him.

"Was there some trouble here?" he asked.

"Look at my bar," the bartender said, almost in tears. "What am I gonna tell Mr. Taylor?"

"You're a little late, sheriff," Clint said. "The excitement's all over."

"What happened?"

"I'm sure your brother can tell you that," Jack First said. "You'll find him over at the doctor's, no doubt."

"My brother?" Sheriff Roby looked down at Tony Dundee's blood, which had made two pools on the floor. "Was he hurt?"

"No," Clint said, "but a friend of his was."

"Friend?"

"Tony Dundee."

"What happened to Dundee?"

"He took a bullet in each leg," Clint said. "It was the only way we could keep him from crushing us without killing him."

"Smart move," the sheriff said. "That damn brother of mine, he can't control Dundee."

"Well, he won't have to for a while," Clint said. "It'll probably be some time before he's walking around again."

"Knowing Dundee," Roby said, "he'll be hobbling around tomorrow. You fellas better make sure he doesn't catch either of you alone."

"Why doesn't he carry a gun?" Clint asked.

"He never learned to use one," Roby said. "He's clumsy." The man held up one of his hands and wriggled the fingers. "Got these real thick fingers. He's more likely to shoot himself than anyone else."

"Sheriff, I'd suggest you tell you brother to stay away from us," Clint said.

"He makes a lot of bad decisions."

"I get the feeling this one was made for him," Clint said. Roby frowned.

"You think somebody put him up to picking a fight with both of you?"

"Why would he do it, otherwise?" Clint asked.

"Like I said," the lawman replied, "he makes a lot of wrong decisions."

"Well, maybe his big brother should watch out for him a little better," First said.

"Believe me," Sheriff Roby said, "I try." He looked around. "Where's Taylor?"

Clint shrugged. "Looks like he took off when all the excitement started."

"Also looks like he's gonna need a new mirror."

"I'm sure he can afford it," Clint said.

"Yeah," Roby said. "I guess he can. You gents try to stay out of trouble, you hear?"

"We'll sure try," Jack First said.

Roby nodded, turned and walked out of the saloon. From

behind him Clint could hear the bartender, still whimpering and wringing his hands over his shattered mirror.

"Oh, for Chissake, Wendell," Annie said, "it wasn't even your mirror. Stop cryin'."

FOURTEEN

They finished the beer Annie had drawn for them, and when Nick Taylor still had not returned, Clint started to get the idea that it was the little gambler who had sent the three men after them.

"If that's true," First said, after Clint had voiced his opinion, "then he must be involved with the vigilantes."

"When we find him," Clint said, "we'll have to ask him."

"And how do we do that?"

"Well," Clint said, looking across the room at Annie, "we do have a connection here. Maybe she can tell us where he lives."

"I'll leave that to you," First said. "I see a connection forming between you two."

"Me?" Clint asked. "You're the young buck here."

"Maybe," First said, "but I suspect she prefers an older stag."

"Thanks."

"You know what I mean," First said. "Besides, I'm not interested, and she can tell."

"This landlady of yours must be something, if you're not interested in someone like Annie."

"I don't know what you mean," Jack First said.

53

"Right," Clint said, putting his empty mug down on the bar. Wendell, the bartender, was still sweeping up broken glass from behind the bar, so Clint didn't bother him. He walked across the floor to where Annie was standing, talking to two men seated at a table. When the men saw Clint approaching, they suddenly found something very interesting in their drinks. Sensing she'd lost their attention, Annie turned and smiled as Clint reached her.

"Can we talk a minute?"

"That's my business," she said, "talkin' to handsome men like you. Come to my corner."

She led him to a corner of the room where they had a little bit of privacy.

"What's on your mind?" she asked.

"Your boss."

"Nicky?"

"I'm finding his absence a bit suspicious."

"I was finding it odd," she admitted, "but why are you finding it suspicious?"

"He made a big production out of welcoming us here, then he disappeared when all the action started."

"You think he sent those boys after you?"

"That's what I'm thinking," Clint said.

"What do you want from me?" she asked. "I can't confirm or deny that."

"I don't expect you to," he said, "but maybe you can tell me where to find him—maybe where he lives?"

"Sure," she said, "and get fired." She waved her arms. "Everybody in the place sees me talkin' to you."

"You have a point," he said. "I'm sorry I asked. I don't want to get you into any trouble."

She looked around, then lowered her voice.

"Where are you staying?"

"The Laredo House."

"Go back to your hotel and wait for me," she said. "I'll come by as soon as I can. We can talk then."

"All right," he said. "Thanks, Annie."

"Now give me some money."

"What for?"

"So it looks like we made a business transaction."

"Oh." He reached into his pocket and held out his hand. "How much?"

"This'll do," she said, nabbing five dollars from his palm. She dropped it between her breasts and smiled up at him. "I'll see you later, Clint."

He nodded, watched her walk away, then went back to rejoin Jack First at the bar.

"What's going on?" First asked. "What did you pay her for?"

"That was just to make people think we were doing business," Clint said.

"And were you?"

"No."

"Did you find out anything about Taylor?"

"Not yet," Clint said. "She's going to come to my room later and help us out."

"Us?"

"With some information."

"In your room."

"Yeah," Clint said. "She doesn't want to get fired, Jack. She's afraid if she told me where he lived here and now everyone would know it was her."

"I see."

Clint looked at Wendell to see if he was in earshot, but the depressed bartender was not interested in anything they had to say.

"I'm going to my hotel to wait for her."

First put down his beer mug with about an inch left at the bottom.

"I'll walk that far with you and then keep on going to my boarding house. I think a soak in a hot tub might keep me from feeling so sore in the morning."

"Good idea," Clint said. "Get that nice landlady of yours to draw it for you."

"She's a lady, Clint," First said.

"That may be," Clint said, "but lady or not, Jack, they're all women."

FIFTEEN

When the knock came at the door of Clint's room, he was fairly sure it was Annie, but he took his gun with him, anyway. He put it behind his back and opened the door. Annie was standing in the hall, looking both ways. She was wearing the same low-cut dress she'd been wearing at work, but had a shawl covering her shoulders.

"Quick," she said, "let me in."

He stepped back to allow her to slip into the room, then closed the door and turned to face her.

"What's behind your back?" she asked.

He brought the gun around and said, "Sorry. Can't be too careful."

"Considering who you are, I understand."

"You know who I am?"

"Well," she said, "your friend the ranger did announce it to everyone in the saloon."

"Oh, right."

"You could have killed all three of those men, couldn't you?" she asked. Actually, it was more a statement than a question.

"I might have been able to," Clint said. "Certainly the ranger and I could have."

"Then why didn't you?"

"There was no reason to."

"But your reputation—"

"You can't believe everything you hear," Clint said, cutting her off. "You're smart enough to know that, Annie."

"Yes, I am." She removed her shawl and dropped it onto the bed behind her. She put her hands behind her back, which seemed to make her breasts swell. She was a small woman, but she was very well endowed. She had breasts and hips that were made for bed. "What was it you wanted to know?"

It took a moment before he remembered what they had been talking about in the saloon.

"Your boss," he said. "I wanted to know where he lives."

"Oh yes, you think he sent those men after you," she said. "Why would he do that?"

"We think it might have something to do with the hanging that happened outside of town."

"You think he had something to do with that?"

"Maybe."

"But why?"

"The ranger and I think that rustler was hanged by vigilantes," Clint explained. "Vigilantes need a leader."

"Nicky Taylor?" she asked. "Little Nicky, the leader of a group of vigilantes?" She started to laugh, and her large, round breasts giggled interestingly.

"Is it that funny?"

"If you knew Nick at all you'd be laughing, too."

"Tell me about him."

"Can I sit on the bed?"

"Sure."

She sat and said, "Little Nicky . . ."

When he heard the key in the lock of his door, Jack Fist reached for his gun, which was hanging on the bed post. He sat up, shirtless, wearing only his jeans and no shoes. His hair was still wet from his bath, which the Widow Connolly had graciously agreed to draw for him. There were a few moments, while soaking in that tub, when he had a fantasy of Mrs. Connolly—whose first name he still did not know—coming into the room, stripping off her clothes and joining him in the bath. When those thoughts caused him to embarrass himself, he pushed them away and got out of the tub.

He pointed the gun at the door, and, as it opened and the Widow Connolly entered, it was almost like a dream coming true.

"Are you going to shoot me?" she asked.

"Do you always enter your guest's rooms with a key?" he asked. "I had no way of knowing it was you."

"Really?" she asked. "No way?"

She closed the door and leaned against it. She was dressed for bed, wearing a dressing gown over her nightgown. Her hair was down and smelled freshly washed, and she was incredibly beautiful. He felt his pulse begin racing faster and faster. He was not that experienced with women, but he knew a beautiful one when he saw one. There was also something about a young, lovely widow that was incredibly sexy.

"I don't understand."

"You don't, do you?" she asked. "You have no idea how endearing that is."

"Endearing?"

She pushed away from the door and came across the room to him. He looked up at her. She ran her hand through his hair, then slid it down to cup his chin.

"How do you feel about bold women?" she asked.

He swallowed. "I don't know. I-I don't think I've ever met one."

"Well, you have now."

She leaned over and kissed him. At first he didn't react, but she moaned and put her hands on him and her mouth was incredibly warm and sweet. Finally—feeling such a fool—he began to kiss her back. Her tongue flicked over his lips and into his mouth, and gently she pushed him down on the bed until she was lying on top of him.

SIXTEEN

"He lives in a room above the saloon," Annie said. "And his office is in the back. He's usually in one place or the other."

"Is there a rear door into the building?"

"Yes, and it leads into the kitchen behind the saloon, and to a stairway that leads upstairs."

"Good, that's good. Does he have a woman?"

"A regular woman? No. But he usually has one of the girls go upstairs with him."

"One of the girls?"

She nodded. "He'll pick one towards the end of the night and tell her to come up."

"So . . . he's done that to you?"

"Yes," she said, "in the beginning, when I first started working there, I was too scared to say no. Then I realized how much money I brought in, and that he wouldn't fire me for saying no."

"So, you're popular?"

"I'm very popular," Annie said. "In case you haven't noticed, I have a very nice . . . personality."

"Oh," he said, staring at her breasts. "I noticed . . ."

* * *

61

Jack First's dream continued to come true when the Widow Connolly stood up and removed both her dressing gown and her nightgown. She stood there in all her glory. Slender, with smooth, dark skin, small but firm breasts with dark nipples, and a dark patch of hair between her legs. The smell of her flesh was intoxicating to him and he was so engorged, he thought he would burst.

"You're nervous," she said, kneeling before him.

"Yes."

"Don't be." She put both her hands on his thighs. "You're going to do fine."

"Yes."

She rubbed her hands up and down his thighs, then unbuttoned his trousers and pulled them off, with assistance from him. When she tugged his underwear down and his penis sprang into view she smiled and almost clapped.

"I knew it," she said, taking him in her hand. "I knew you'd be beautiful. Big, and hard, smooth and beautiful."

"I-I don't know what to say . . . I . . ."

"Don't say or do anything, my darling," she said, taking him in both hands. "I'll do it all."

She bent and took him into her mouth, and he thought that nothing had ever felt as hot, or as good . . .

"Are you going to go looking for him tonight?" Annie asked.

"No," Clint said, "not tonight."

"What were your plans for tonight, then?"

"I didn't have any," he said. "I mean, other than going to bed. It's been kind of a long day."

"For me, too," she said. "Do you mind if I join you?"

"You mean, in bed?"

"Yes," she said. "I mean in bed."

She reached up to her shoulders and tugged her dress down until it was bunched around her waist. Her breasts absolutely fell into view. They were large, pale, with heavy undersides. Her nipples seemed high up, and they were the color of pennies.

"No," he said, his mouth dry, "I don't mind at all."

He knelt down in from of her and took a breast in each hand, cupping them underneath, hefting them, enjoying their weight and smoothness in his palms and then lifting them to his mouth so he could kiss and suck her nipples, then nibble them, causing her to sigh and moan and lean back on her hands . . .

Jack First tenderly kissed the Widow Connolly's breasts, holding them in his hands as if he were afraid he'd break them.

"I'm not fragile, darling," she said. "I promise I won't break."

"I'm sorry," he said, "I've just never seen anyone so . . . beautiful."

"Oh my God," she said. "You're so sincere."

"Is that bad?"

"No, lover," she said, "that's good . . . but right now I don't want to talk, anymore."

She reached between them, took hold of his rock-hard penis and urged it toward her moist pussy.

When the tip of his penis pierced her, Jack First couldn't hold himself back. He drove himself deeply inside of her and then began to pound away at her mindlessly . . .

Clint quickly divested himself of all his clothes while Annie removed her dress the rest of the way. She scooted up to the top of the bed and he eagerly joined her there, taking her into his arms and pulling her opulent flesh closer to him. He filled his mouth and his hands with her flesh as she writhed against him. Finally, she managed to secure the top position, smothering him with her breasts while she lifted her hips and then impaled herself upon him.

"Yesssssss," she hissed as she began to ride him desperately . . .

•   •   •

"Wow," the Widow Connolly said, rolling away from Jack First and then turning to look back at him.

"I'm sorry," he said, breathlessly. "Did I hurt you?"

They were both drenched in perspiration, and she swore she had felt the bed move across the floor. She wondered if any of the other boarders had been able to hear them.

"It takes you a while to get going," she said, "but when you do. . . . Wow!"

He wiped his hands over his face and they came away soaking wet. The young man had never lost control of himself that way before.

"I'm sorry," he said, again. "I hope I didn't—"

"Darling, hush," she said. She scooted up against him again and put her finger to his lips. "You didn't hurt me at all. Quite the contrary. I don't think I've ever felt that . . . good in my whole life."

"Oh," he said, and then added, "me, neither."

"You're such a serious young man," she said, sliding her hand down over his belly. "I think it was a good thing for you to lose control like that, don't you?"

"I-I'm not sure—"

"Well, I am," she said. She moved her hand lower and seized him, shocked at how hard he was.

"Are you still hard?" she asked. "Or just again?"

Looking embarrassed he said, "Again."

"All right, then," she said, putting her lips to his neck, right near his ear. "Again it will be."

She slid one leg over him and mounted him that way, but he gripped her by the elbows and said, "Wait."

"What is it?" she asked. Her eyes were glazing over, already, and her mouth was puffy from their kisses.

"I can't keep thinking of you as the Widow Connolly," he said. "What's you name?"

She laughed and said, "Kathy, Ranger Jack . . . my name is Kathy."

SEVENTEEN

Annie rolled over in bed the next morning and banged into Clint with her chunky buttocks.

"Hey!" he said.

"Sorry," she said. "I'm not used to sleeping with another person."

"Sleeping?" he asked. "Is that what we've been doing?"

She giggled and said, "Well, I admit we haven't really done much of that, have we?"

"No."

She reached her hand beneath the sheet, took hold of him and began to stroke him. His body responded immediately.

"And do you want to sleep now?" she asked.

"Truthfully? Yes . . ."

She slid her finger along the underside of his penis and when she came to that tender, sensitive spot just beneath the tip he jumped and said, ". . . and no."

"I didn't think so."

She slithered beneath the sheet so that he couldn't see her at all, but he felt her wrap her lips around him and engulf him in her hot, wet mouth.

He wondered if he'd ever sleep again with her around . . .

* * *

Jack First woke before Kathy Connolly did and spent the better part of half an hour just watching her sleep. When she woke she looked up at him, smiled and stretched.

"Good morning," she said.

"Good morning."

"How do you feel?"

"Wonderful," he said. "Better than I've ever felt in my life."

"Well, that's very good."

"How are you?"

"I'm just fine" she said, "but I have to go downstairs and make breakfast for the house."

She stood up and he watched her pad naked across the room to retrieve her nightgown and dressing gown. Her hair stood out from her head wildly, and they both had both red marks on their skin and bruises.

She came to the bed and kissed him tenderly.

"You're my wonderful beast, Jack First," she whispered to him.

He watched as the door closed behind her, leaving him with a terrible sense of loss. He'd been with women before, but had never felt like this. He wondered if he was in love.

But wonder as he might about that, there was one thing he knew for sure—he was hungry, and she was going downstairs to make breakfast.

He got out of bed and poured some water from a pitcher into a basin. He felt his face and wondered if he should shave.

Clint had to push Annie out of his bed—something he'd never envisioned he'd ever have to do.

"Am I the first woman you've ever kicked out of bed?" she asked, dressing.

"Yes," he said, "definitely. But I'm old now, and you're trying to kill me."

"Oh," she said, leaning over him, "not so old, Mr. Adams. I'm a little worn out, myself."

"Well, get out of here and let me get at least an hour of sleep," he said.

"Will I see you tonight?" she asked. "You're not leaving town, are you?"

"I don't think I am," he said. "I certainly wouldn't leave without saying good-bye, so one way or another I'll see you in the saloon, later."

"All right," she said. "I'm going to hold you to that."

"Away," he said, pulling the sheet over his head, "I have to get some sleep . . ."

He was snoring as she went out the door.

EIGHTEEN

Before splitting up the night before Clint and Jack First had agreed to meet for breakfast at the same café they'd eaten steaks at. Actually, Clint was going to have breakfast there. First was going to eat at his rooming house, and then meet Clint at the café.

Clint entered the restaurant on rubbery legs and was greeted warmly by Angela, the waitress.

"I was waiting for you to show up," she said. "Steak and eggs?"

"Sounds good."

She flashed him a big, white smile and went into the kitchen. If he hadn't spent the entire night with Annie he would have been much more interested in Angela.

The waitress was very flirtatious with him throughout his meal, and he knew he was not being receptive to her. He was being nice, but was not quite flirting back. He felt bad and was relieved when Ranger Jack First entered and joined him at the table.

"Breakfast, ranger?" she asked.

"I already ate, thanks," First said. "I'll take coffee, though."

"Comin' up."

When she left Clint asked, "What happened?"

"What do you mean?"

"You look different this morning."

"Different?"

"Yeah."

"I . . . don't know what you mean."

Clint peered closely at the young man.

"Ranger First, are you blushing?"

First sat back, scowled angrily and said, "No!"

"You are," Clint said. "You're blushing. Something tells me you and the Widow Connolly did more than talk last night."

"What makes you think it was Kathy—"

"Ah ha," Clint said. "Kathy. When did you get on a first-name basis with the widow?"

"None of your—"

"I'll tell you when," Clint went on. "Last night, that's when." Then he leaned forward and asked, "Is that a bruise on your face? That wasn't there last night. I know you've got some bruises, but that one . . . I don't think that came from being thrown behind the bar."

Instantly, the ranger's hand went to his face. Angela came back at that point with a cup for First and poured him some coffee.

"Where'd you get that bruise?" she asked, touching his face gently.

He turned bright pink this time and Angela laughed and said, "Oh, excuse me," which only made it worse.

Clint finished the last of his breakfast and shoved the plate away from him.

"Okay, that's enough humiliation," he said. "Whatever you did last night is your business. However, what you're going to do today is mine. But before we start, how are you really feeling after last night?

"Pretty good," the ranger said. "The hot bath last night really helped. I'm a little sore, but nothing too bad."

"Okay, then. What did you have in mind for today?"

"Start talking to the ranchers, I guess."

"Can I make a suggestion?"

"Go ahead."

"I think we should start with the owner of the WX spread, Frank Waxman."

"The man those three cowboys from last night work for?"

Clint nodded.

"Supposed to be the biggest rancher in this area."

First shrugged and said, "Might as well start at the top. But before we leave, I want to check in at the undertaker and make sure the sheriff brought the body in."

"Okay," Clint said, "we can do that first. I also think we should find Nick Taylor today and have a talk with him, too."

"Well, either he sent those men after us last night, or their employer did."

"Or their boss."

"What?" First asked. "I thought Waxman—"

"He pays their wages, but they work for the foreman, like on any other ranch. He might have given the orders."

"Then we should find out who the foreman is."

"When we meet the owner," Clint said, "we'll probably meet the foreman."

"What if we split up?" First suggested. "You go find Taylor and I'll go talk to Frank Waxman."

"Not a good idea," Clint said. "The point was for us to watch each other's back, remember? I don't think either one of us would have walked away from that encounter last night alone."

"You would have," First said.

"What makes you say that?"

"You wouldn't have taken a beating from that man if you were alone, and I think all three of those cowboys would have ended up going to see the doc—if not dead."

"I can't tell you you're wrong," Clint said. "Facing them

alone I probably would have used my gun. The point is, we managed to get through it without killing anyone. We worked as a team and I think we should keep doing that."

"All right, then," First said. "Let's ride out to the WX and see what we can find out."

NINETEEN

As expected, Clint and Jack First were greeted at the WX spread by the foreman, Ben Pearson. Pearson had spent the night before chewing out his three men when they came back to the ranch, with Dundee patched up but useless for work . . .

"What were you thinkin'?" Pearson demanded of the three of them. He pointed his finger at Marty Roby. "I blame you. These two idiots follow you."

"Boss, it was just—"

"Who put you up to it? Hmmm?" Pearson demanded. "Whose bright idea was it for you to brace the Gunsmith and a Texas Ranger."

"We knew about the ranger," Roby said, in self-defense, "but we didn't know the other man was the Gunsmith."

"We sure didn't," Gaylord Horn said. "I never would've agreed no matter how much we got pa—"

"Shut up!" Roby snapped, but it was too late.

"Oh, so you got paid for this little bit of craziness?" Pearson asked. "How much?"

Horn looked at Roby. Tony Dundee wasn't there. He was

lying on his bunk inside the bunkhouse while this conversation took place right outside.

"Gaylord, go to bed!" Pearson snapped.

"Right, boss."

Pearson waited while Horn opened the door, entered the bunkhouse and closed the door behind him.

"Who was it, Marty?"

"Little Nicky."

"What did he pay you to do?"

"He gave us twenty dollars a piece to poke at the ranger, see how good he was."

"And you found out, didn't you?"

"If it wasn't for the Gunsmith, Tony would have taken that ranger apart," Roby insisted.

"And that made you right?" Pearson demanded. "If Mr. Waxman hears about this, the three of you will be out on your asses."

"You ain't gonna tell him, are you?" Roby asked.

"What am I supposed to tell him about Tony?" Pearson demanded. "How do I explain a bullet in each leg?"

Roby shrugged. "Tell him Tony finally picked on the wrong fella."

"That'd be true, wouldn't it?" Ben Pearson said. "That'd be damned true!"

"You ain't gonna tell him, are ya, boss?" Roby asked, again.

"Go to bed, Marty," Pearson said.

"What are you gonna say?"

"I'll figure somethin' out."

"Thanks, boss."

"Yeah."

Roby went inside and Pearson stood with his hands on his hips. He'd heard the shots last night from the window of his whorehouse, but he didn't find out what had happened until later, when Nick Taylor met him there and told him.

"Guess it wasn't such a good idea, eh, Ben?" Little Nicky said.

"It wasn't ours, Nick," Pearson said.

"What do we do now?"

"Don't let Adams find you," Pearson said. "Not for a while."

"What about the ranger?"

"Don't worry about the ranger," Pearson said. "Clint Adams is the one to worry about . . ."

Clint and First reined in their horses and dismounted in front of the foreman.

"Are you Ben Pearson?" First asked.

"That's right," Pearson said. "I'm foreman here."

"So we heard in town," First said. "I'm Jack First, Texas Rangers, and this is Clint Adams. We'd like to see Mr. Waxman."

"What's it about?" Pearson asked. "I usually handle all ranch business. Is this about the fracas last night at the saloon?"

"You heard about that, did you?" Clint asked.

"Sure I did," Pearson said. "My men told me, when they brought Tony Dundee back here with a bullet in each leg. Was that really necessary?"

"I guess not," Clint said. "I guess we could have just killed him. Either way we weren't about to take a beating from him."

Pearson laughed. "He would have crushed the two of you."

"Is that what he gets paid to do?" Jack First asked.

"He gets paid to be a ranch hand," Pearson said. "What he does in town is up to him, and however much he drinks. The boys were just havin' some fun. That's what I heard."

"Well, it wasn't fun for us," Clint said.

"Anyway," First said, "that's not what we want to see Mr. Waxman about."

"What then?"

"Murder," the ranger said. "We'd like to see him about murder."

TWENTY

Pearson made them wait a good fifteen minutes while he went inside to talk to Frank Waxman. When he showed them to the man's office they found him seated behind his desk, a white-haired, barrel-chested man who was something of a South Texas legend.

"You gents wanted to see me?" Waxman asked. He did not rise, or offer to shake hands.

"Sir, my name is Jack First, I'm a Texas rang—"

"I can see that from your badge, Ranger," Waxman said. He looked at Clint. "And you're the Gunsmith?"

"My name is Clint Adams."

Waxman looked back at the ranger.

"The Gunsmith is riding with the rangers now, young fella?" he asked.

"Mr. Adams is simply assisting me in my inquiries, sir," Ranger First responded.

Clint smiled and said, "The rangers are a little short-handed, right now."

"What kind of inquiries?" Waxman asked First, ignoring Clint.

First turned and looked at Ben Pearson, who was standing in a corner of the room, observing.

"Ben is my foreman, and my right hand," Waxman said. "Whatever you want to say to me you can say in front of him."

"Very well," First said. "I'm sure you heard about the lynching that took place just outside of town?"

"I heard somebody hanged a rustler," Waxman said. "What's that got to do with me?"

"How do you feel about that, sir?"

"Somebody deserves a medal," Waxman said. "That fella was making life miserable for every rancher in these parts."

"That one man?"

"He was the leader," Waxman said.

"And you think lynching him will put a stop to the rustling?" First asked.

"I think it's possible," Waxman said. "Look, let's cut to the chase, here, Ranger. The word is going around that vigilantes did the hanging. Are you out here to ask me if I had anything to do with it?"

"Yes, sir," First said. "That's why I'm here. I'm asking you, and I'll be asking all of the other ranchers in the area the same question."

"And I'm supposed to feel less offended because of that?" Waxman asked.

"Mr. Waxman," Clint said, "I don't think we're really worried about you being offended."

Waxman looked at Clint, then back at the ranger.

"Is he here officially?" the rancher asked.

"Sir," First said, "he's here as officially as your foreman is. Could you answer the question?"

"Am I a vigilante?" Waxman asked. "Is that the question?"

"Or do you know anyone who is?"

"If I was a vigilante, Ranger," Waxman said, "do you think I would admit to it?"

"Probably not."

"Definitely not!" Waxman said. "Why would I be that stupid?"

"Sir," First said, "why would you be stupid enough to even leave me with any doubt? If you don't answer, I'll be left with no alternative but to suspect you."

"The law had its chance to take care of this matter," Waxman said, "and failed miserably. Whoever strung that rustler up did us all a favor. Do I know who did it? No. Did I do it? No. Do you have any other questions I can answer?"

Clint very deliberately looked over at Ben Pearson.

"What about you?" he asked.

"What about me?" Pearson asked.

First turned his head to look at the foreman. Clint had been very careful to keep the man in view at all times.

"Same questions," the ranger said.

Pearson looked at Waxman.

"Answer them, Ben, so we can get back to business."

"No."

"No what?" First asked.

"No, I'm not a vigilante, and no, I don't know anyone who is. Anything else?"

First looked back at Waxman.

"You knew what we'd say, Ranger," the rancher said. "You came out here to observe our reactions, so what have you concluded?"

"Nothing right now, sir," First said. "I'll reserve my conclusions for another time. Thank you for your time."

"That's it?"

"Yes, sir," First said. "Thank you for your time."

"Just for the record," Waxman said, "I hope you don't find out who the vigilantes are."

"Why is that, sir?"

"Because I'm afraid there'll be some pretty decent people beneath those masks."

"Who said anything about the vigilantes wearing masks?" Ranger First asked.

"Give me a break, Ranger," Waxman said. "Vigilantes always wear masks—otherwise they're just a lynch party."

"I'm sorry, sir," First said, "but I don't see the distinction."

TWENTY-ONE

They followed Ben Pearson though the house to the front door, but as they reached it, the door opened and a very attractive woman entered. She looked about forty, but wore it very well. Her hair was blond, her skin pale and smooth, and she was tall and slender. She might have been out riding because she was wearing a pair of jeans and a man's shirt, and was carrying a flat-brimmed hat in her hands. Her hair was long, and looked windblown.

"Oh, Ben," she said, coming up short when she saw the three men coming at her. "I didn't know we were having company today."

"Neither did we, Mrs. Waxman," the foreman said. "This is Texas Ranger First and Clint Adams. They came to talk to Mr. Waxman about vigilantes."

"Oh?" She gave Clint a quick glance, then looked directly at Jack First. "And what made you think my husband would know anything about vigilantes, Ranger?"

"I'm questioning all the ranchers in the area, ma'am," First said. "Your husband just happens to be the first one."

"First because he's the biggest?"

"Yes."

"And what conclusion did you come to?"

"Your husband asked me the same question," the young ranger said. "I haven't come to any conclusions, yet."

"And you, Mr. Adams?"

"It's really not my job to come to conclusions, Mrs. Waxman. That's the ranger's job."

"Then why are you here?"

"I'm just helping Ranger First stay alive during his investigation."

"Do you have reason to believe someone would try to kill the ranger?"

"Yes, ma'am," Clint said. "The reason was hanging from a tree outside of town when I first arrived."

"But that man was guilty of cattle rustling."

"He didn't receive a trial, ma'am," First said. "He was hanged illegally."

"And it's your job to find out who did it?"

"Yes, ma'am."

"Well, I wish you luck, then," she said. "Ben, is Frank still in his office?"

"Yes, ma'am," the foreman said. "I was just showing these gents out."

"Good day to you both, then," she said to Clint and First, and moved past them. All three men turned and watched her walk until she disappeared down the hall that led to her husband's office.

"Very attractive lady," Clint said.

"If you say so."

"Somewhat younger than her husband, though."

"That's their business," Ben Pearson said. He pointed. "There's the door, gents."

"Thank you, Mr. Pearson," First said.

Clint and First went out and pulled the door closed behind them.

"What do you think?" First asked as they descended the steps.

"I think the three of them were particularly determined to be unhelpful. I also think that's what we'll get from all the other ranchers."

"Still," First said, "I have to talk to all of them. It's got to be done."

"Did you notice anything about the foreman and the lady of the house?" Clint asked.

"Like what?

"Like hot glances?"

"Hot glances?" First looked confused.

"A young woman married to an older man, with a handsome foreman just a few years younger than her?"

They mounted up before First asked, "You think they're . . . involved?"

"Just pointing out a possibility."

As soon as the door closed behind them, Leslie Waxman reappeared from the hallway and joined Pearson in the foyer.

"What did they want?"

"Just what they said they wanted," Pearson said.

"How did Frank do?"

"He did fine," Pearson said. "We do have a problem, though."

"Oh? What?"

"Your friend."

"My . . . friend?"

"Taylor."

Leslie Waxman smiled.

"Little Nicky? What did he do?"

He explained about sending the three hands after Clint Adams and Jack First and the outcome.

"That was stupid," she said.

"Yes."

"I'll have to have a talk with Nick."

"Just a talk?"

She tapped his cheek and said, "Don't be so jealous, darling. I don't bother you about your little whore, do I?"

She turned and this time did walk down the hall to her husband's office.

TWENTY-TWO

Clint and First spent the remainder of the day riding to other ranches in the area, asking the same questions and watching for reactions. By the time they got back to town, it was dusk. They left their horses at the livery and went to one of the other saloons in town for a beer to cut the dust, preferring to stay away from Little Nicky's, at the moment.

"Well," Clint said, rubbing both hands over his face, "that didn't accomplish much."

"I wouldn't exactly say that," First said from across the table.

Clint took a couple of swallows of his cold beer and peered across the table at the young ranger. They were in a small saloon off the main street, and there were only a few other bored-looking men sitting at tables or standing at the bar, and an equally bored-looking bartender. No one seemed particularly interested in them.

"What do you think we accomplished today?"

"Well," First said, "everybody in the county knows you're working with me now."

Clint stared at First in disbelief.

"Ranger," he said, "I do believe that's the first joke I've heard you make."

•   •   •

In Nick Taylor's room above Little Nicky's Saloon, Leslie Waxman rolled off of Nick Taylor's naked form and laughed.

"God," Taylor said, "you're beautiful. I ever tell you that before?"

"All the time, lover," she said.

Taylor stared at her, admiring the small, brown-tipped breasts and the freckles between them.

"I have to go," she said. "He'll be wondering why I'm so late."

She stood up and started getting dressed. He propped himself up on his pillows and watched her. He didn't know how he'd gotten so lucky. Saloon girls used to be good enough for him, but not since he'd met Leslie Waxman.

"When are you gonna leave him?"

"Leave who? Frank?"

"Do you have another husband?"

She got into her unmentionables and then pulled on her jeans, looking over at him.

"Why would I leave him, Nicky?" she asked. "He's got all that money."

She was the only one who could call him Nicky without his temper flaring up about it.

"What about love?" he asked.

She put her shirt on and buttoned it.

"That's exactly what I'm talking about, Nicky," she said. "I love his money."

"Then divorce him," he said. "You'll get some of his money that way."

"I don't want some of his money, darling," she said. "I want all of it. I've told you that before."

"I can take care of you, Leslie," he insisted.

"I don't want to be taken care of," she said. "The whole point of my marriage was to get enough money to take care of myself."

"Well, when is that going to happen?" he asked. "Frank has to die for you to get all his money. He's not that old. He's still got some good years left in him."

"Don't worry about me, Nicky," she said, pulling her boots on to finish dressing. "I can take care of everything myself."

"What do you mean by everything?"

"Never mind," she said. "There's something else we have to talk about before I leave."

"What?"

"That stunt you pulled last night with Roby, Horn and Dundee," she said. "You might have gotten them killed."

"What do you care?" he asked. "They work for your husband, not you."

She sat on the bed and looked him in the eyes.

"It was stupid, Nick. We don't need somebody like the Gunsmith poking around here."

"What about the ranger?"

"I think I can handle the young ranger."

He reached out and gripped her arm.

"The way you handle me?"

"Is that what I do, Nick? Handle you?"

"Isn't it?" he asked. "Isn't that what you do with all men? Like Pearson?"

"What about Ben?"

"Are you sleeping with him, too?"

She pulled free of him and stood up.

"I don't answer to you, Nicky."

"Leslie," he said, as she headed for the door, "I'm sorry."

She stopped at the door and looked at him.

"Just don't do anything stupid anymore, Nick," she said. "Don't do anything to ruin everything."

"I won't," he said. "I promise. When can I see you again?"

"I'll let you know," she said. "Good night, Nick."

"Good night, Leslie."

She went out and he walked to the window to look down at the street. He didn't see her, because she used the back door when she came and went.

TWENTY-THREE

Clint and First decided they should finish the day up by talking with Nick Taylor of Little Nicky's Saloon. Remembering what Annie had told him about the back door, Clint led the ranger to the rear of the saloon. As they approached the door, it opened and they had only a moment to hide themselves behind some crates. They watched as a woman came out, looked around carefully, then pulled the door closed behind her and hurried to the nearby alley that would take her to the street.

"Was that who I thought it was?" Clint asked.

First nodded and said, "Frank Waxman's wife. And you thought she and the foreman were doing something together."

"Just because she's sleeping with Nick Taylor doesn't mean she's not also doing something with Ben Pearson. A woman who looks like that could have lots of men and could be controlling them all."

"You think she's the leader of the vigilantes?"

"It's too early to jump to that kind of a conclusion," Clint said. "Why don't we see what Little Nicky has to say to all of this?"

They went to the back door, found it unlocked and went into the building.

When the knock came at the door Nick Taylor thought Leslie Waxman was coming back for more of "little" Nicky.

"Couldn't stay away, huh?" he shouted, bounding off the bed and answering the door naked. When he saw the two men standing there he backed up abruptly and tried to close the door.

"Not so fast, Nicky," Clint said. "We've got some questions for you about last night."

"I don't have time—"

"Sorry we're not who you thought we were," Jack First said, "but she left, we saw her."

"You . . . saw who?"

"Mrs. Waxman," Clint said.

"I don't know—"

They stepped inside and closed the door behind them.

"Put something on, Nick," Clint said. "We're not interested in what you have to show us."

Abruptly, Taylor put both hands in front of his crotch, then started looking around for his clothes. When he located them he hopped around, trying to get them on. Briefly Clint considered making the man remain naked, but while that probably would have made him feel more vulnerable, it wouldn't have done anything for Clint and First. Better to have the man cover up.

"Sit on the bed, Nick," Clint said. "If there's a gun around here don't think about going for it."

"My weapon of choice is a deck of cards, gents," Taylor said. "I don't usually bother with guns."

"Not when you can send other men to do your dirty work for you, huh?" First asked.

"Is that what this is about?" Taylor asked. He put his hands out, palms up and said, "That was a joke."

"Your joke almost got a man killed," Clint said. "You didn't stick around to see it."

"I had business elsewhere," Taylor said. "Look, I'm sorry if you got hurt, Ranger—"

"How did you know I got hurt if you weren't around to see it?" First asked.

"I . . . heard later what happened," the smaller man said. "I heard that Tony hurt you, and then the two of you shot him in the legs. That was pretty smart—"

"We don't need your compliments, Nicky," Clint said.

Taylor closed his eyes and said, "My name is Nick, not Nicky."

"You don't like being called *Nicky*?" Clint asked.

"No."

"What does Leslie Waxman call you, *Nicky*?" Clint asked.

"What would Mr. Waxman call you if he heard about you and his wife?"

"If he was able to satisfy her, she wouldn't be coming to me," Taylor said. "And my name is *Nick*."

"I kind of like *Nicky*," Clint said, looking at First. "What about you?"

"Little Nicky kind of fits him better," First said.

"If you don't like being called Nicky," Clint asked, "why'd you call the saloon *Little Nicky*?"

"That's different," Taylor said. "That's the name of the business, it's got nothing to do with me."

"Looks to me like it has everything to do with you," Clint said, "but let's forget about that for now. We want to know why you sent those men after us last night."

"I told you, it was a joke."

"What made you think of it?" First asked. "Two strangers come into your place and you decide to play a dangerous joke on them?"

"I just—"

"I think you wanted to test us," Clint said, "see how much we'd take, see how we'd react to the situation. Either you wanted to see the result, or someone put you up to it."

"I don't work for anybody else," Taylor said. "I'm my own boss."

Clint studied him for a few moments, then looked at Jack First and said, "I don't think that's the case, do you?"

First studied Taylor for a few moments, and then said, "No, he just doesn't look that smart."

"Somebody put you up to it, Nick," Clint said. "Who was it?"

TWENTY-FOUR

"It was my idea, nobody else's," Nick Taylor said. "Admittedly, it wasn't a smart thing to do. How about I just apologize to the both of you and we move on from there?"

"Move on to where?" First asked.

"Why don't we go downstairs and I'll buy both of you a drink," Taylor proposed.

"I don't think so, Nicky," Clint said. "We still have some things to discuss up here."

Taylor closed his eyes, took a deep breath and said, "We're not gonna get anywhere if you keep calling me Nicky."

"Why not?" Clint asked. "What are you going to do? Hit me with a deck of cards?"

Nick Taylor stood up from the bed and drew himself up to his full height of five six.

"Sit back down, Nicky," Clint said.

"Look—"

"Sit down, Mr. Taylor!" Jack First snapped.

The gambler sat.

"Tell us about vigilantes."

"Ranger," Taylor said, "I don't know anything about vigilantes. Why would you think I do?"

"Because you seemed like a smart man to me," First said. "Maybe I was wrong."

"Not wrong about me being smart," Taylor said, 'but that doesn't mean I know anything about vigilantes. You'd do well to talk to all the ranchers in the area. They're the ones who had a beer with the cattle rustler, not me.'

"We've done that," First said. "We talked to the ranchers today, and they all say the same thing."

"They had nothing to do with it."

"Right."

"And you believed them?"

"Some of them are telling the truth," First said.

"And some aren't."

"Can you tell us which ones aren't?" Clint asked.

"I told you," the gambler said. "I don't know anything about vigilantes."

"Guess," Clint said.

"What?"

"You know the men in this area," First said. "They come to your saloon. You interact with them. Take a guess. Who do you think is the leader of these vigilantes?"

"The leader?" Taylor asked. "That would have to be somebody with an axe to grind, somebody smart, somebody men would listen to and follow."

"Who are you describing, Mr. Taylor?" First asked.

"Sounds like Frank Waxman to me," Nick Taylor said, "but I could be wrong. You asked me to guess, and that's my educated guess."

"That guess would carry more weight with me," Clint said, "if you weren't sleeping with the man's wife."

Outside, on the street, at the mouth of another alley, Leslie Waxman found Ben Pearson waiting for her where they agreed he would be waiting with two horses.

"Well?"

"He won't do anything stupid again," she said.

"You guarantee?"

"Pretty much."

"But you had to sleep with him to get him to agree," Pearson said, angrily.

"Darling, I had to sleep with him to get his attention," she replied, touching his face. "Come on, we have to get back or Frank will start to wonder."

She moved towards her horse but Pearson grabbed her, turned her roughly and kissed her, his hands roaming over her. She didn't resist, but kissed him back. The kiss went on for a long time and when it ended they were both breathless.

"That make you feel better, Ben?" she asked.

"You can't keep me at arm's length forever, Leslie," Pearson said. "Sooner or later I'm going to have to choose between you and Frank. You're gonna have to give me some damned good reasons to pick you over him."

"I'm working on that, darling," she said, preparing to mount her horse. "I'm working on it."

"Sleeping with Leslie has nothing to do with it," Nick Taylor insisted. "Frank Waxman is a leader of men, pure and simple. If the men of this county were going to follow someone, it would be him."

"We'll take your guess under advisement, Mr. Taylor," Jack First said.

"Are we done here?" Taylor asked. "I have a business to run."

"We're finished," Jack First said.

Taylor stood up.

"I have to go downstairs," he said. "My offer of a drink still stands."

"No thanks, Nicky," Clint said. "I think we'll do our drinking somewhere else."

"Keep pushing me, Adams," Taylor said. "You'll find I'm lethal with something other than a deck of cards."

"Somehow I doubt that, *Nicky*," Clint said.

TWENTY-FIVE

"You pushed him pretty hard," Jack First said when they reached Clint's hotel.

"I don't like him."

"Why not?" the ranger asked. "Because he's sleeping with a married woman?"

"Why would I care about that?" Clint asked. "They're both adults. They can sleep with whoever they want. Why? Is that the part that bothers you?"

"Well . . . yes," First said. "I mean . . . it's not right."

"Well, if there's blame, it's on her, don't you think?" Clint asked. "After all, she's the married one."

"But he knows she's married," First said. "He's just as much to blame. It's just not . . . moral."

"I think you're going to have to modernize your thinking if you're going to survive, Jack."

"I'm sorry," First said. "I just don't think it's . . . right."

"Well, you can't arrest him for it," Clint said. "I don't even think a judge would care—especially when there's a murder to be solved."

"I suppose you're right," First said. "I should keep my priorities straight."

"And right now your priority should be getting a meal

and some rest so we can start over again tomorrow."

"I guess you're right," First said. "To be honest, I'm not sure what tomorrow will bring. I'm a Texas Ranger, not a detective."

"You've done everything right so far as I can see, Jack," Clint said. "Go get something to eat and we'll talk about the next step tomorrow."

"What are you going to do?"

"The same thing," Clint said, "only not in the same places."

First looked crestfallen.

"I really thought we'd come out of today knowing something definite, Clint."

"We would have needed somebody to confess for that, Jack," Clint said. "We'll just have to work a little harder at it."

"I'll have to send my captain a telegram tomorrow, advising him of my progress."

"Tell him an arrest is imminent," Clint said. "How will he know the difference?"

"You mean lie to him?"

"Not exactly lie," Clint said, "just not the whole truth."

First looked like he wasn't sure about it.

"Goodnight, Jack," Clint said. "See you tomorrow."

" 'Night, Clint."

As First started to walk away, Clint decided he'd better walk the younger man to his rooming house.

"Wait, up, Jack," Clint said. "I want to make sure you get there safe. We poked a lot of people today. One of them might decide to poke back."

TWENTY-SIX

"That's the last one," the man said, entering the barn and pulling the door closed behind him.

"All right, then," the leader said. "We're all here."

In the barn were twenty men, all wearing masks so that their faces were hidden, and their voices were muffled. Three of the men knew each other and had arranged for all the other men to attend the meeting. The masks kept the other seventeen men from knowing who the organizers were, who the leader was, and who each of the other men were.

"Settle down," the leader called. A raised platform had been formed out of hay bales, so that he was standing high enough for everyone to see him.

"Quiet down!" one of the other men said. He was standing on one side of the leader, and the man who had locked the barn door was standing on the other side.

Gradually, the talking fell off and the group quieted down.

"I've asked you all here because we have a problem."

"Another one?" someone shouted. "We gonna stretch somebody else out?"

Several men turned to him and told him to shut up.

"Listen up!" the leader shouted. "We hanged one man

who deserved it, and we won't hang another unless we find another member of the gang of rustlers that's been hitting us."

"They won't be comin' around anymore," a man called from the back. "We gave them a lesson they won't forget!"

"That may be true," the leader said, "but we have another problem besides rustlers."

"And what's that?" someone asked.

"The law."

"We don't have nothin' to fear from ol' Sheriff Roby," somebody said.

"It's not Roby," the leader said. "I don't know how many of you know this, but we have a Texas ranger in town. He came here looking for Fernandez, the rustler."

"Well," a disembodied voice called out, "somebody did his job for him."

"That may be," the leader said, "but now he's trying to find out who hanged the rustler. Seems the ranger doesn't believe in vigilantes."

"Whether he believes in us or not," a man said, "we're here."

"And he's determined to find us," the leader said, "and arrest us."

"He's just one man!" came a cry from the crowd.

"There's just one ranger, that's true," the leader said, "but he does have help."

"Who?"

"Clint Adams."

There were a few moments of hushed silence, and then someone said, "The Gunsmith."

"That's right. Some of you may have already seen him around town. He's apparently backing the ranger up."

"A ranger and the Gunsmith," someone said.

"That's still only two men," someone else said.

"But one of them is the Gunsmith!"

Men began to shout back and forth and the leader decided

to let them tire themselves out. He leaned down so that his two sidekicks could come close.

"Want us to quiet them down?" one asked.

"No," the leader said, "they'll wear each other out."

"Sombody's gonna go off half-cocked after this," the second man said. "That's for sure."

"That may be," the leader said. "Luckily, none of them has seen our faces, so if they do something foolish and get caught, it won't come back to us."

The other two men nodded and one said, "That's true."

"I'll give them a few more minutes, and then warn them not to do anything."

"That's all somebody's gonna need to do just the opposite."

"I know," the leader said, "I'm counting on that."

TWENTY-SEVEN

Clint went back to the café for a steak dinner and found Angela still waiting tables there.

"Do you work all day?" he asked.

"All day," she said, "for another half hour."

"Looks like I just made it."

"Steak?"

"Yep."

"I'll make sure it gets going before Art puts out the flame in the stove. I'll also bring some coffee over."

"Okay, thanks."

He watched her walk to the kitchen, then leaned back and took a deep breath. All of the ranchers had seemed fairly offended by the suggestion they might be vigilantes. One or more of them had to be faking, though, and one or more of them might decide to do something drastic either during the night or tomorrow. When they had parted company at the rooming house, Clint had warned Jack First to be particularly alert during the night. He intended to follow his own advice, as well.

Jack First sat at the kitchen table and watched Kathy Connolly putter around the kitchen, preparing him something to eat. He'd apologized for missing dinner when he entered, but didn't even have to ask if he could have something. She offered to feed him.

"You must have put quite a few miles on your horse today," she said, "you and Mr. Adams."

"We did ride over quite a bit of ground."

"Did you find out anything helpful?"

"We talked to all the ranchers," he said, "and they all denied being involved with vigilantes."

She came to the table with a bowl of beef stew and set it before him with a hunk of homemade bread.

"Did that surprise you?" she asked.

"Of course not," he said. "This looks and smells wonderful."

"There's more if you want it."

"I think I will."

She sat down opposite him, looked him in the eye and said, "There's more of everything if you want it."

He knew what she meant and couldn't stop himself from blushing.

"Ranger Jack," she said, smiling at him, "I think that blush is one of your most endearing qualities. Don't ever lose it."

"Mrs. Connolly," he said, "I don't think I'll have any choice in the matter."

Clint ravenously destroyed his steak, sitting alone in the small café. Angela and Al were going about getting the place closed up for the night, and by the time Clint was done, so were they.

"Good night, Angela," Al said, as he left. He never said a word to Clint, who thought that Angela had probably forced him into making that one last steak dinner.

" 'Night, Al."

She closed and locked the front door behind him.

"Seems like I've held everything up," Clint said. "Least I could do is walk you home."

"Well," she said, "that would be very nice. Let me just clear away your plate and I'll be ready to go."

Clint actually helped her carry his plates and cup into the kitchen, where she left them, saying she could clean them in the morning.

They left the café together, and she locked the door behind them.

"Al never walks you home after closing?" he asked, as they strolled along.

"No," she said, "there's not an ounce of chivalry in Al. Luckily, he's a great cook."

"That he is."

"Did you and the ranger find out anything about the vigilantes today?"

"How did you know about that?'

"It's all over town, what happened last night at Little Nicky's, and what the two of you have been doing."

"Is that a fact?" he said. "I wonder who it is has been spreading it all over town."

"Stuff spreads like wildfire around here without much help at all," Angela told him.

"Like any town, I guess."

"The sheriff's not gonna be very helpful to you, is he?"

"He's got to live and work in this town," Clint said, "and even if he doesn't know who's behind the vigilante masks, it's bound to be some of his neighbors. It'll be up to outsiders like the ranger and me to pull the masks off and bring them to justice."

She hesitated, then looked at him and asked, "Must you?"

"What?"

"Bring them to justice?"

"Well," Clint said, "the must comes from the ranger. He's the one stuck on seeing that justice is done."

"And you?" she asked. "What are you stuck on?"

"On keeping him alive so he can do it," Clint said. "You see he's young and kind of headstrong, and he's got a captain who sent him here by himself. I get the feeling there's lots of testing going on here. I think the rangers are testing young Jack, and I think Jack is testing himself. I just intend to see he passes every test."

"Why?" she asked. "Are you friends?"

"We didn't even know each other before yesterday," Clint said, "but right now I'd have to say yes, we are friends—and I'd go through a lot for a friend."

"This is me," she said, stopping them in front of a two-story clapboard building. She touched his arm and said, "I get the feeling you're a good friend to have, Clint Adams."

"Do you need a friend, Angela?"

She studied him a moment, then said, "Maybe. Maybe I do. I'll let you know."

She started for the stairway alongside the building, went up two or three steps, then turned around to face him.

"I'd invite you in for coffee, but I'm just bushed from working all day."

"That's all right," he said. "I'm bushed from riding all day."

"Good night, then. Thanks for walking me home."

"Good night, Angela," he said. "It was my pleasure."

TWENTY-EIGHT

Three men were left in the barn when the others had left—
the leader, and his numbers one and two—and they all removed their masks because they knew each other. One of
them broke out a bottle of whiskey he'd been hiding, and
they sat on hay bales and passed it around. It wouldn't do
for the three of them to be seen in a saloon together.

"I don't know whether our meeting tonight will accomplish what we want it to," the leader said.

"How do you mean?" Number Two asked.

"The men we have are followers, not leaders."

"That's what we wanted," Number Two reminded him.

"I know that," the leader said, "but for this situation I
think we might need some men who can think for themselves."

"If that's the case," Number One said, "we're shit out of
luck in this town."

"Yeah," Number Two said, passing the bottle, "we'd need
men who can think for themselves and who can handle a
gun. Where are we gonna find men like that?"

"Not in this town," Number One said, accepting the bottle, "that's for damn sure."

"I agree," the leader said, waiting his turn for the bottle.

"That's why I think we're going to have to import some talent."

"Hire somebody?" Number One asked, passing the leader the bottle.

"Yes."

"More than one somebody," Number Two said.

"I'm glad we're of like minds on this," the leader said.

"Yeah," Number One said, "we might be of like minds, but we ain't of like wallets."

"We can split the cost of hiring some men in such a way that each of us is satisfied," the leader said.

"Who are we gonna hire?" Number Two asked.

The leader passed him the bottle and wondered if his numbers one and two were going to be able to get home tonight without falling off their horses.

"I've got somebody in mind," he said, "and all we have to do is pay him and he'll bring his own men with him."

"Who we talkin' 'bout?" Number One asked.

The leader took the bottle, pretended to drink and then passed it back.

"Let me worry about that," he said.

"You gonna hire a professional gunny," Number One said. "We better be careful we don't bring in a worse problem than what we got."

"Don't worry," the leader said, "the man I have in mind only kills for money. Once he's paid he'll move on."

"I gotta get home," Number Two said. "My wife'll skin me 'live."

"Mine, too," Number One said.

"Very well," the leader said. "We'll call this meeting of the Laredo Vigilantes adjourned."

TWENTY-NINE

The next day Clint suggested to Jack First that maybe they should question all the ranchers in the area and not just the four biggest, as they had the day before.

"That could take days," First said.

"You got something better to do?" Clint asked.

First scratched his head and said, "I suppose not."

"So we'll spend two days questioning the other ranchers," Clint said. "By that time somebody should decide to try something to get rid of us."

First looked surprised.

"So you figure we should just stay around, be targets and wait for someone to come after us?"

"Again," Clint again, "do you have something else to do? Or a better idea?"

First thought a moment, then said, "Neither."

"I rest my case," Clint said.

So for the next two days they rode from ranch to ranch, speaking even to the owners of the smallest spreads in the county. While the large ranchers had reacted indignantly, feeling they were being accused of vigilantism, the smaller ranchers simply reacted with either amazement, or boredom. It was Clint's opinion that none of them had anything to do with what was happening. They had enough problems trying to keep their businesses going without taking the time to go riding around the county wearing a hood.

Three days later Clint and First were sitting in a small saloon together, sharing a beer. They had taken to using this place to sit and discuss the day's events. The bartender was also the owner and appreciated their business, since most of the townsmen drank and gambled at Little Nicky's. The small saloon was called The River Lady, for some reason.

"Better than naming it after myself," the bartender had said when Clint asked about the name.

"What's your name?"

"Barney," the man said. "Can you imagine me callin' this place Little Barney's?"

They couldn't, so The River Lady it was.

"Okay, so we've talked to all the ranchers in the area," First said, wearily. "What did we accomplish, except for riding to hell, goin' all over the county?"

"We're making people nervous."

"You think so?" First asked.

"Look," Clint said, "they tested us that first night we were here, and we passed. They're going to figure their next move very carefully."

"And how are we going to figure our next move?"

First seemed depressed, and Clint was wondering if the young man had had enough and was ready to ride out.

"Jack," he said, "we can always give up. Your original assignment was the rustling. Fernandez is dead, and there seems to be a lull in the rustling because of it. The vigilantes got what they wanted. There's no reason to believe they're going to hang somebody else."

"They don't have to hang anybody else," First maintained. "They've already broken the law once, and that's all it takes."

"So you're still determined to bring them to justice?"

"I'm determined that they should be brought to justice," First said, speaking very carefully, "I'm just not sure that I'm the Texas Ranger to do it."

"Well, I'm sure you are."

"What makes you so sure?"

"You want it," Clint said. "This is more than just a job to you, Jack. I haven't known a lot of badge toters who feel the way you do. To a lot of them it's just a job. To you it's a calling."

"That makes me sound like a . . ."

"A what?"

"Zealot."

"I'm not even sure I know what that means," Clint said, "but I can guess. All it means is that you take your badge serious, Jack. There's nothing wrong with that."

"The last telegram from my captain says I have two more days to show some results, or I'm to return to Austin."

"Two days," Clint said. "Okay, that's not bad. Maybe we should go have another talk with Sheriff Roby."

"What for?"

Clint shrugged. "Just to push him a bit. After all, his brother was one of the three who braced us that night. Maybe he's also one of the vigilantes. Let's go see how the sheriff feels about that."

"Might as well," First said. "We're not accomplishing much sitting here."

"Let's go walk the streets with a bull's-eye painted on our backs," Clint said. "Maybe that'll accomplish something."

They headed for the door and when they reached it, Ranger First stopped abruptly.

"What's wrong?" Clint asked.

"All of a sudden," First said, "my back itches."

"Welcome to my world," the Gunsmith said.

THIRTY

When they walked into Sheriff Roby's office, it was obvious he wasn't a happy man.

"You're not glad to see us, Sheriff," Clint said. "I think I can understand that."

"I expected you to be here for a day or two," Roby said. "It's goin' on what? Four? Five?"

"Well," Clint said, "at least there hasn't been any trouble since that night your brother tried to start some. You must have had a talk with him about it."

"My brother don't do what I tell him," Roby said. "As for trouble, you been talkin' to every rancher in the county, accusin' them of being vigilantes, and I been hearin' about it. Ain't you ready to give up yet and leave town?"

"No," Jack First said, "not yet, Sheriff. I'll be ready to leave when I have the men responsible for hanging Fernandez."

"That damned rustler?" Roby snapped. "He's been more trouble dead than he was alive!"

"You can help us, you know," Clint said. "Get us out of your hair, stop us from harassing your citizens."

"Just tell me how."

"Tell us who the vigilantes are," First said.

Roby stared at him as if he were crazy.

"I can't do that."

"Why not?"

"Because . . . I don't know who they are."

"Come on, Sheriff," Clint said. "Maybe you don't know who the leaders are, but you've got to know some of the faces behind the masks. What about your brother?"

"My brother?" the sheriff asked in amazement. "Even if he was a vigilante, why would you think I'd tell you?"

"Okay, then how about . . . Tony Dundee, or somebody like . . . Nicky Taylor."

"Dundee and Taylor," Roby said, shaking his head. "You think wearing a mask would keep their identities a secret? Dundee's as big as a tree and Taylor . . . well, he ain't called Little Nicky for nothin'."

"Come on, give us something, Sheriff," Clint said, "something we can work with. It'll get us out of your hair, and nobody will know it came from you."

Roby seemed to waver, and for a moment Clint thought the strategy was going to work and he was going to give them at least one name.

"Come on man," Jack First said, picking an unfortunate time to speak, "do your job."

His words seemed to dispel the moment and Roby became stubborn again.

"I'm sorry, but I can't help you," he said.

"You're the sheriff."

"This is my home," Roby said, "and these are my neighbors. I'm not gonna turn them over to you because they made one mistake."

"Well, that's interesting," First said.

"What is?" the lawman asked.

"Are you saying that this was the first act of vigilantism in Laredo?" the ranger asked.

"Yes," the sheriff said, "I thought you knew that."

"No," First said, "nobody mentioned that."

"Tell me this, Roby," Clint asked, "do you think it will be the last act?"

"That would be up to the rustlers, I guess," Roby said. "I haven't seen or heard of any since Fernandez got strung up. That should tell you something."

"I'll tell you something I've learned about vigilantes, Sheriff," Clint said. "Once they get a taste of power, of what they can do, they tend to like it, and want to do it again. They'll be looking for an excuse to string somebody else up."

"I think you're wrong," Sheriff Roby said. "I think this is a one-time thing and if you'll ride off and leave us alone it'll go away."

"I don't think you really believe that, Sheriff," Jack First said, heading for the door, "I don't think you can be that naïve."

As he went out the door Clint looked at Roby and said, "I do."

THIRTY-ONE

"He's a fool," First said, outside. "He is that damn naïve, isn't he?"

"I think he's just hopeful," Clint said. "He wants it all to go away by itself so he won't have to deal with it."

"Is he just bad at his job?" the ranger asked. "Or is he being paid by the ranchers?"

"Maybe he's just worried."

"About what?"

They both looked at each other then and had the same thought, only it was Clint who said it.

"His brother."

They decided that the sheriff either knew his brother was one of the vigilantes, or he thought he was. Either way he'd try to protect him, especially since he was the older brother. They went to the livery, mounted their horses and once again rode out to the WX spread to ask Marty Roby some questions.

"Hey, boss," a ranch hand called out to Ben Pearson, "two riders comin'."

Pearson peered off into the distance and thought he recognized the two men.

"Now what do they want?" he asked himself. He turned to the other three men he was in the corral with. "Keep workin', I'll be right back."

"Looks like that Texas Ranger," Gaylord Horn said, "and the Gunsmith."

"You especially stay here," Pearson said. "I don't want any more trouble from you."

"Sure, boss."

Pearson left the corral and managed to head off Clint and Jack First before they reached the front of the house.

"Mr. Waxman ain't around," Pearson announced to them, "so you're out of luck."

"As a matter of fact we're not here to see Mr. Waxman," Jack First told him.

"Well, I got nothin' to tell you," Pearson said.

"Not you, either," Clint said, "or Mrs. Waxman for that matter. We're looking for Marty Roby."

Pearson frowned. "What do you want with Marty?"

"Just some questions," First said. "Where is he?"

"He's workin'," Pearson said. "This is a workin' ranch, that's what we do here."

"That's fine," First said. "We won't keep him long. Just tell us where he is and we'll ask our questions and be gone."

Pearson frowned again and Clint wondered if the man was going to lie.

"Okay," the foreman said finally, "he's in the stable. I've been givin' him shit jobs to do since his stunt the other night. He's got to pick up the slack for Dundee, until the big man gets back on his feet."

"Yeah, well," Clint said, "that was unfortunate."

"Don't keep him long," Pearson said, pointing toward the stable. "He's got the work of two men to do."

"We understand," First said.

They both turned their horses and rode towards the stable. When Pearson turned to go back to work he saw Leslie Waxman waving to him from the front door, so he walked over to see what she wanted.

"What about him?" First asked, as they rode toward the stable.

"He's a possibility," Clint said. "He's a foreman, which means he's got leadership qualities. I guess we could talk to him a bit more before we leave. Let's concentrate on Roby, right now."

They reached the stable, dismounted and walked their horses inside.

Pearson reached the front porch and mounted the steps.

"What are they doing here?" she asked.

"They want to talk to Marty Roby."

"About what?"

"Vigilantes, I guess."

"Maybe it's just about the other night?" she asked.

"It's all about vigilantes, Leslie."

"They didn't want to speak to Frank?"

"No," Pearson said, "they specifically said they were not here to talk to Mr. Waxman."

She tapped a front tooth with a fingernail and said, "Tell Mr. Adams I'd like to talk to him before he leaves."

"About what?"

"I just want to feel him out," she said. "I didn't get much of a chance to talk to him when we met."

"What are you gonna tell him, Leslie?"

"I don't know, Ben," she said, "but I think around the ranch you should keep calling me Mrs. Waxman, don't you?"

He stared at her and then said, "Whatever you say, Mrs. Waxman."

"Good," she said, "just ask him to come to the house when he's done."

"Should I bring him in?"

"No," she said, "just tell him to knock on the door."

"Whatever you say," he replied, again. "You're the boss's wife."

"Yes," she said, "I am."

THIRTY-TWO

When Marty Roby saw both Clint and Jack First enter the stable he lifted the pitchfork he was holding and held it out in front of him.

"Hey, hey," he said, "I ain't wearin' a gun. I don't want no trouble with you two."

"We're not here for trouble, Marty," Clint said. "The ranger just has some questions to ask you."

"About what?"

"Put the pitchfork down, Marty," First said. "You're not going to need it with us."

Warily, Roby first lowered the pitchfork and then dropped it to the ground.

"Wouldn't do me no good against your guns, anyway," he said. "Whataya want?"

"Just a talk," First said.

"Is this about the other night?" Roby asked. "I told you, we was just funnin'. I'm sorry it happened, 'cause I been havin' to do my work and Dundee's work for days now."

"That's too bad," Clint said.

"We had a talk with your brother today," First said.

"My brother?"

"The sheriff."

121

Roby made a noise and said, "Some sheriff Al is."

"What do you mean?" First asked.

Roby opened his mouth to answer, then thought better of it.

"Never mind," he said. "I just ain't crazy about badge toters, and my brother turns out to be one."

"Marty," Clint said, "the sheriff is not cooperating with us, and the ranger thinks he might be trying to protect you."

"Protect me? From what?"

"From the law."

"I don't need protection from the law," Roby said. "I ain't done nothin'."

"Really?" Clint asked. "Your brother seems to think you might be one of the vigilantes."

"What?" Marty Roby was aghast. "He said that?"

"Not in so many words," Clint said.

"Huh?"

"He didn't actually say that, but he's not doing his job."

"My brother only does his job when he's told to."

"Told by who?" First asked.

"Whoever's got the money,"

"Are you saying the law's for sale in Laredo?" Jack First asked.

"Cheap," Roby said.

"So you're not one of the vigilantes?" First asked.

"I don't like vigilantes," Marty said. "They think they're better than everybody else."

Marty Roby didn't like lawmen or vigilantes. His friends must have simply been ranch hands, like Horn and Dundee.

"Marty, let me ask you something," Clint said. "Do you think your brother could be one of the vigilantes?"

"Al?" He gave the question some thought. "If there was money in it," he finally said.

"Vigilantes don't get paid," First said.

"Yeah," Clint said, "it's sort of like being a volunteer fireman."

"Well then, that leaves Al Roby out," Marty said. "He don't do anything for free."

"Why would he take the job as sheriff, then?" First asked. "It certainly can't pay much."

"It don't matter what it pays," Marty said, "Al Roby will make it pay for him."

"You don't have a very high opinion of your brother," First said, "and it doesn't seem to have anything to do with him being sheriff."

"You're right," Marty said, "it doesn't. It has to do with the fact that he's greedy . . ."

". . . and he doesn't share," Clint finished for him.

Marty smiled and said, "Exactly."

They walked their horses back out and Jack First said, "Well, it seems to me there's more of a chance of Al Roby being a vigilante than Marty Roby."

"If he could find a way to make it pay," Clint said.

"How would hanging a rustler pay off?" First asked.

"I don't know. . . . Look who's coming."

Ben Pearson was approaching them with a purposeful stride.

"Adams."

"Yes?"

"Mrs. Waxman would like a word before you leave."

"Is that a fact?" Clint asked. "Where is she?"

"Up at the house," Pearson said. "Just knock on the door."

"What does she want?"

"She didn't say," Pearson replied. "I'm just the hired help."

Clint looked at First. "I better see what the lady wants."

First put his hand out for Eclipse's reins.

"I'll wait here."

"Be back soon."

Clint started for the house, hoping First would take the opportunity to talk with Ben Pearson.

THIRTY-THREE

When Leslie Waxman answered Clint's knock at the door, she took his breath away, she was that beautiful. Her long hair was down, and she smelled as if she was fresh from a bath.

"Mr. Adams," she said. "How nice."

"Your foreman said you wanted to talk to me."

"Yes, I do," she said. "Would you come in, please?"

He entered and she closed the door.

"Is your husband at home?"

"No," she said, "he's across the border in Mexico."

"Doing business?" he asked.

"I assume so. I really don't keep track of my husband's business, so he doesn't confide in me."

Clint wondered if Frank Waxman's business had anything to do with vigilantes. It really did make sense for the rancher to be the vigilante leader. He had the most to lose to rustlers.

"Please," she said, "have a glass of sherry with me in the sitting room."

He smiled and said, "It's your party."

"I wonder what she wants," First said to Pearson as Clint walked away.

"I don't know," Pearson said. "Did you get what you wanted from Marty?"

"Not exactly."

"What were you looking for?" Pearson asked. "Maybe I can help."

"Would you?" First asked. "Would you help, if you could?"

"That depends on what you want."

"I want justice," First said. "I want the men who hanged a man without benefit of a trial."

"A rustler."

"Yes," First said, "a rustler, but he deserved a trial."

"He would have been found guilty and sent to prison," Pearson said. "Or would he?"

"I guess we'll never know," First said. "He'll never know. He was robbed of that right."

"What about the robbing he did?"

"No one had the right to kill him," First said. "No matter what he did."

"Couldn't you look at it as self-defense?"

"Could you?" First asked. "Could you really make a case for self-defense for a group of masked men who strung him up from a tree?"

Pearson looked away. Was he ashamed?

"Tell me, Mr. Pearson," First said.

"Tell you what?"

"A name. Just one name, that's all I need. No one will know you gave it to me."

"What the hell? You think I know the names of the vig-ilantes?" the foreman asked.

"Maybe," First said. "Maybe you do. Even if the name you know is . . . your own?"

Leslie Waxman handed Clint a glass of sherry and invited him to sit down.

"Is this meant to be a long visit, Mrs. Waxman?" he asked, remaining standing.

"Please," she said, "call me Leslie."

"You wanted more from me than just to share a glass of sherry, Leslie," he said. "What's on your mind?"

"Actually," she said, "I was wondering what was on yours."

"Vigilantes."

"Is that all?"

"At the moment."

She laughed.

"You're alone with a beautiful woman and all you can think of is vigilantes?"

"There's no doubt that you're beautiful," Clint said, "but you're also married."

"But my husband is not here."

"That doesn't make you any less married." He set his glass down on a nearby table. "If you brought me here to try to seduce me, you're wasting both of our time."

She smiled and said, "No, I didn't ask you here to seduce you. I'm afraid I was just . . . playing."

"Games are a waste of time, too."

"I love my husband, Mr. Adams," she said. "I want to know if you mean him harm."

"I don't mean anyone any harm, Leslie," he said. "Not if they're innocent, that is."

"And who is innocent, anymore?" she asked.

"I'm not here to debate you."

"You won't be seduced, and you won't debate," she said. "Just tell me what you want?"

"I want the vigilantes," he said. "I want one name."

"One?" she asked. "That's all you need?"

"It'll be a start."

She thought a moment, then said, "Then I just might be able to help you, after all."

THIRTY-FOUR

When Clint came out of the house, he saw Ben Pearson walking away from Jack First, who was standing there holding both horses. He and Pearson passed each other, but the foreman never looked at him. He had a scowl on his face Clint could not read.

As Clint reached First the ranger handed him Eclipse's reins.

"What'd she want?" he asked.

"She's a game player, that one," Clint said.

"I thought she was a lady."

"A lady is still a woman," Clint said, "and they're all game players."

"Then why does it surprise you that Mrs. Waxman is, too?" First asked.

"It doesn't, really," Clint said. "I just think she's especially good at it."

"So what did she say?"

Clint looked around. Pearson had walked over to the corral where some of his men were working with some horses. From where they stood Clint recognized one of them from the saloon the night they shot Tony Dundee in the legs.

"Let's mount up and ride out," Clint said. "We can talk on the way back to town."

They rode out and Clint kept looking behind them to make sure they weren't being followed.

"So what'd she have to say?" Jack asked.

"After she realized I wasn't going to play games she wanted to know what I was going to do to her husband."

"What'd you say?"

"I told her I was interested in vigilantes," Clint said. "Said if I got a name to work with I probably wouldn't be doing anything to her husband—providing he didn't have anything to do with the vigilantes who hanged Fernandez."

"How did she react?"

"She's a practiced liar," Clint said. "We saw her coming out the back door of Little Nicky's. She plays with men, Jack, and with the truth."

"Doesn't really sound like much of a lady, then. Did she give you a name?"

"She did. She said—"

"Before you tell me," First said, cutting him off, "Pearson and I did some talking, too."

"What'd you get out of him?"

"I got a name, too," First said.

"How'd you manage that?"

"I just asked him."

"Doesn't seem the type of man to just answer a question straight out."

"Well, I told him I needed a name . . . even if it was his."

Clint looked over at the young ranger, impressed that he'd taken such a direct approach.

"How did he react to that?"

"Guess he didn't like it that much," First said. "He told me he wouldn't have anything to do with vigilantes."

"But he knew somebody who might?"

"He said he'd be willing to guess, if that was all I

wanted," First said. "As long as I understood it was just a guess."

"That's about the way Mrs. Waxman put it," Clint said.

"Kind of a coincidence, eh?" First asked.

"Probably not," Clint said. "What was the name you got from Pearson?"

"Nick Taylor."

"Yep," Clint said. "That's the name she gave me, too."

"Another coincidence?"

"Maybe," Clint said. "Maybe not."

THIRTY-FIVE

Frank Waxman was in Nueva Laredo, just across the river from Laredo, in a little cantina with no name. He was sitting with a bottle of tequila when three men walked in. He knew one of them and waved him over to the table. The man walked over while the other two went to the bar and ordered two beers.

Waxman had two glasses in front of him and a half full mug of beer. As the man sat down he opened the bottle of tequila for the first time and poured out two glasses.

"Hello, Earl."

"Mr. Waxman."

"Have some tequila."

"Thanks."

It took Roy Earl some time to sit down because he was so tall. He had to come down from that great height in order to get his butt into a chair. He picked up the glass and drained it, set it back down so Waxman could refill it. Waxman drank his and washed it down with some beer.

"Been a long time, Mr. Waxman."

"Yeah, it has," Waxman said.

"I just figured you ain't had a need for me and my talents for—what, five years?"

"Closer to six."

"Six, then."

Earl picked up his glass and drained it again, set it back down. Waxman filled it.

"When I got your telegram I figured things had changed, though."

"Somewhat," Waxman said. "I'm set up pretty well across the border in Laredo."

"That a fact?"

"But I might have some trouble."

"You only used to call for me when you definitely did have trouble," Earl said.

"Okay," Waxman said, "I definitely have some trouble."

"What kind of trouble?"

"The Texas Ranger kind."

Earl started twirling his third glass of tequila round and round on the table.

"That's the serious kind," he said, "and the expensive kind."

"It gets more expensive."

"More expensive than the law?"

"I'm afraid so."

Earl drank down the third glass, turned it upside down and put it down on the table.

"That kind of expense usually means a big name."

"The biggest."

"It's soundin' more and more interestin', Mr. Waxman."

Waxman sat back.

"You've put on some weight, Roy."

"Comes with age, Mr. Waxman," the gunman said. "I'm all of forty-four now."

"Yeah, well," Waxman said, "I know about putting weight on with age. I'm sixty-four, myself."

"You look pretty good for a man that age."

"You as good as you used to be, Roy?"

"I'm better than I used to be, Mr. Waxman," Earl said. "Better and more expensive."

"Money's no problem," Waxman said.

Earl sat back and stared across the table at the older man.

"We talkin' Wild Bill Hickok here?" he finally asked.

"Pretty near."

Now Earl sat forward.

"Say it."

Waxman hesitated, then said, "Clint Adams."

Earl sat back again.

"The Gunsmith," Waxman added.

"I know who Clint Adams is."

"So, are you in?"

Earl looked over at the two men standing at the bar. Both were in their thirties, good boys as long as you told them exactly what you wanted them to do.

"Tell me about the ranger."

After they had worked out all the details Frank Waxman was the first man to leave the cantina. He went outside and got into his buggy. It had been many years since Waxman had sat on a horse. He didn't even do it anymore during round up.

He drove out of Nueva Laredo and headed back to the WX spread.

After Waxman left, Roy Earl got up and walked to the bar. As he got there Leo Wells handed him a beer.

"We got a job?" Josh Whitman asked.

"We have a job," Earl said.

"Where?" Leo asked.

"Laredo."

"Good money?" Josh asked.

"Great money."

"What do we got to do?" Leo asked.

"How do you boys feel," Earl asked, "about killing a Texas Ranger?"

THIRTY-SIX

Clint and First rode back into Laredo and went directly to the livery.

"I'm going to rub Eclipse down myself," Clint told First as they dismounted. "Take some time to think."

First decided to do the same with his horse, so they unsaddled them together.

"Think we should talk to Nick Taylor again?" First asked.

"You know, I discussed him with Annie that first night. She doesn't think he has it in him to be a vigilante. I think I trust her judgment and opinion more than Leslie Waxman and Ben Pearson's right now."

"What about the sheriff and his brother?"

"I'm thinking Sheriff Al is a more likely vigilante than brother Marty," Clint said. "Maybe we need to take a look around his office, or wherever he lives."

"You mean break in?"

"That's what I mean."

"I can't be caught breaking into a lawman's home, Clint," Ranger Jack First said.

"Well, the trick there is not to get caught," Clint said. "He can only be in one of those places at a time."

"No, I mean—"

"I know what you mean, Jack," Clint said, interrupting him. "We can work it out so that I break in while you keep watch."

"What are you expecting to find?"

"I don't know," Clint said. "Something that will give us some answers."

"And who else's home would you be wanting to break into?"

"Well," Clint said, gesturing with the brush he was using to comb through Eclipse's coat, "now that you ask, Frank Waxman's—although that would be a little harder to do. There are a lot of people on that spread at any given time."

"Jesus," First said, "I never thought I'd have to break into people's homes to uphold the law."

"Sometimes you've got to break the law to uphold it, Jack," Clint said.

"That's hard to swallow."

Clint stopped brushing the horse and turned to face the younger man.

"How long have you been a Texas Ranger?"

"Two years."

Clint frowned. "That's actually a lot longer than I thought. You should be more jaded by now."

"Why do I have to become jaded at all?"

"Well," Clint said, "it's either that or go crazy."

"Is upholding the law such a hard thing to do?"

"Yes."

"How long did you do it?"

"I actually wore a badge quite a bit in my twenties," Clint said. "How old are you now?"

"Twenty-six."

"Yeah, I guess it was around there I started to wonder about it."

"I'm not wondering, yet."

"Oh, no?" Clint asked. "What if we have to ride away from here day after tomorrow with nobody paying the price for Carlos Fernandez's death? What will you think then?"

"Somebody has to pay," First said.

"What if nobody does?"

The ranger turned to stare at him with a puzzled expression on his face.

"Somebody has to!"

Clint pointed his brush at First and said, "You're in for a rude awakening, my friend—if not this time, then next time, or the time after that, but very, very soon."

THIRTY-SEVEN

Clint and First were walking down the main street when they saw Frank Waxman driving a buggy up the street towards them.

"He's still the logical choice," Clint said, "but we better concentrate on the sheriff first."

"We have to find out where he lives," First said.

"I think I know who to ask about that."

Waxman nodded to them as he passed, and they nodded in return. He continued on until he drove right out of town.

Clint and First went to Little Nicky's Saloon. They weren't looking for Nick Taylor, but Annie.

"She'll have some of the answers we want," Clint said, as they leaned on the bar.

The bartender came over and said, "What'll you have?"

"I haven't seen you here before," Clint said.

"I'm new," the man said. "The old bartender got fired—something about breakage."

"Well," Clint said, "we wouldn't know anything about that, would we, Jack?"

"Uh, no," Jack First said, "nothing."

"Two beers, please," Clint said.

"Comin' up."

While waiting for the beer Clint turned to look the place over. There were three girls working the floor, but none of them were Annie. He suddenly became worried that maybe Annie had been fired, as well. Maybe Nick Taylor had found out that she'd been talking to him.

When the bartender brought the beers, Clint said, "Annie working tonight?"

"She should be down soon," the man said. "Seems like she's the big draw in this place."

The barman walked away before Clint could comment.

"See what you did?" he said to First.

"What?" the ranger asked. "What did I do?"

"You broke the mirror," Clint said, "and got the poor bartender fired."

"I broke the mir—" First started, then suddenly realized that Clint was joking.

"There, see? You got it. Your sense of humor is developing."

"I'll bet you're glad Annie didn't get fired, too," First said.

"She took a chance talking to me."

"She'll take another chance today, too."

"We'll try and make it look like she's working," Clint said. "Let's just enjoy our beer until she comes down."

Outside of town Frank Waxman sat in his buggy, waiting for the man he was supposed to meet. He was satisfied with his meeting in Nueva Laredo. Roy Earl might just be the man to finally take down Clint Adams, the Gunsmith—and this was a good time for the legend to fall.

He turned in his seat when he heard a rider coming. The sun glinted off the hunk of metal the man wore on his chest. Finally, Sheriff Al Roby reined his horse in next to the buggy.

"How did it go?" Roby asked.

"We're all set," Waxman said. "Roy Earl should be in town later today, with two men."

"Think he can take the Gunsmith?"

"I think he can," Waxman said, "but more importantly, he thinks so. His other two men will handle the ranger."

"Good."

"You know," Waxman said, "once the ranger is dead the Texas Rangers might send another man—or more than one."

"We'll deal with that when the time comes," Roby said.

"Deal with it how?"

Roby sat back in his saddle.

"Okay," he said, "I might as well tell you now. The rangers won't be sending anyone because I'm gonna take down the man who kills the ranger."

"You're going to turn on Earl and his men?" Waxman asked. "Isn't that dangerous?"

"This is all dangerous, Frank," Roby said, "but no, I'm not gonna turn on Earl. I've got somebody else in mind."

"You're going to frame somebody?"

"I'm not gonna frame anybody," Roby said, "I'm gonna blame somebody, and see that they pay for it. Believe me, the rangers will be satisfied with the outcome."

"You've got it all figured."

"Don't I always?" Roby asked. "I told you years ago, with my brains and your money we'll go far."

Waxman remembered the conversation. At the time he'd been as fooled as everyone else by Al Roby's public persona. Once he realized how smart Al Roby really was he'd had no problem throwing in with him.

"Go back to the ranch now, Frank," Roby said, "and don't come to town until I send word that Adams and the ranger are dead."

"I saw them in town, just now."

"Yeah, they're still asking questions all over town and the county," Roby said, "but their time is about up."

"I hope you're right."

"I'm always right, Frank," Roby said. "Remember that."

THIRTY-EIGHT

When Annie came down the stairs all the men in the place noticed. For her part, she noticed Clint standing at the bar and didn't have eyes for anyone else. She walked straight up to him, smiled at Ranger First and took Clint's arm.

"I missed you," she said. "You haven't been around much lately."

"We've been real busy."

"You're here now," she said. "That's what counts. Are you here for business or pleasure?"

Clint hesitated a little too long before saying, "Pleasure."

She dropped his arm abruptly and said, "Liar. You have more questions."

"Just a few," he said. "Don't be angry."

"I'm not," she said, with a pout. "I'm hurt."

"I'll make it up to you, Annie."

"You better," she said. Then she sighed. "All right, go ahead and ask your questions."

"I've got one main one," he said. "Where does Sheriff Roby live?"

She frowned. "Why do you want to know that?"

"I want to pay him a social call."

She studied him curiously, then said, "He's got a small

house at the south end of town. The town gave it to him when he won the election. All the sheriffs have lived there. It's white with yellow trim. Hideous. You can't miss it."

"Does he have a wife?"

"No."

"A girl?"

"Oh, no," she said. "When he wants a girl he comes here and pays for one."

"Annie," Clint said, "two people have given us one name as their guess for who's running the vigilantes."

"I hope it's not me."

"It's Nick."

"Let me guess," she said, "one of those people was Leslie Waxman, right?"

"How'd you know that?"

"She plays with men, Clint," Annie said, "and Nick is one of them, only he can't see it. If she's giving you his name, she's got her own reasons for it. Who else?"

"Ben Pearson."

"Another one of her projects," she said. "He's probably jealous of Nick. Take my word for it, Clint. Nick has nothing to do with vigilantes."

"Okay, Annie," Clint said. "We're done with the questions."

"Good," she said, "then you can start making it up to me right now—upstairs."

Clint looked at First and shrugged. They couldn't do anything until after dark, anyway.

"When the lady's right," he said to the ranger, "the lady is right."

THIRTY-NINE

They left the saloon in time to see Sheriff Roby entering his office, across the street.

"We're in luck," Clint said. "You keep an eye on him and I'll go and check his house."

"W-wait, what do I do if he leaves his office?"

"Follow him."

"And if he goes to his house while you're still inside?"

"Then warn me."

First's eyebrows went up. "How am I supposed to do that?"

"Figure out a way." Clint patted the young ranger on the back. "I have faith in you."

"Clint wait—" First said, but Clint was already hurrying away towards the south end of town . . .

Of course, before leaving the saloon Clint had gone upstairs with Annie to her room to "make up" with her. She led him by the hand up the stairs while most of the men watched, wishing they were him.

Once inside her room she got rid of her dress very quickly and ran her hands over her opulent curves while giving him a smoldering look.

He gathered her into his arms, enjoying the solid feel of
her body, then lifted her and carried her to the bed. He de-
posited her on it, then took his time removing his own
clothes while she watched. When he was naked, and his
erection was standing like a flagpole, she reached for it, fon-
dling and bringing it to her cheek. She rubbed it across her
face, flicking her tongue out to tease it and then stopped
playing and simply engulfed it with her mouth.

She began to suck him, her head bobbing up and down
on him while he held her there with one hand, his eyes
closed and his head thrown back. She sucked him loudly,
the sound just serving to inflame him even more, and
abruptly she released him from her mouth, grabbed him and
pulled him down onto the bed.

"Just lie there," she said. "The only way for you to make
up for disappointing me is to let me have you."

"I'm all yours."

She smiled, mounted him, grabbed his dick in one hand
and guided it between her legs. She was so wet he pierced
her easily as she sat down on him, taking him all the way
in. Then she began riding him, her hands flat on his chest,
her head tossed back, rising up and then coming down on
him and grinding . . .

If this was what she meant by him having to make it up
to her, then he had to disappoint her more often . . .

Clint pushed the recent memory of sex with Annie from his
mind as he reached the sheriff's house. She was right. It was
hideous. However, since this was the house the town gave
whoever was sheriff, he doubted that these were Roby's
choice of colors.

He decided to try the back door, not wanting to be seen
on the lawman's porch. When he reached it, he looked
around, saw no one, put his shoulder to the flimsy door and
then simply forced it open. It was easy. You'd think a lawman's house would be more difficult to break into.

Once inside he paused to allow his eyes to get used to the semidarkness. There was still some light outside, but there was none inside and he dared not light a lamp.

Once he felt he was able to see, he started looking around—not sure what he was looking for, but open to anything. He found many drawers that were empty, and there was obviously no feminine touch here.

There was a second floor and when he found the room Al Roby slept in, he finally found something useful in the bottom drawer of a chest of drawers. In fact, he found quite a few somethings—enough so that he thought it safe to take one, figuring Roby would never miss it. He stuffed it into his pocket, hurried back downstairs and out the back door, which he was able to close behind him since forcing it had left it undamaged.

FORTY

Jack First stood nervously across the street from the sheriff's office. This was not what he had signed up to do when he joined the Texas Rangers. He certainly didn't think he'd be watching another lawman while another man broke into the lawman's house. And Clint was going to want them to break into the office next—which, somehow, felt even worse to him.

He looked up and down the street, wondering what he'd say if someone asked him what he was doing. There was no activity across the street at the sheriff's office and he had a sudden panic attack that maybe the sheriff had gone out a back door while he was watching the front. Maybe he did that from time to time and snuck off home while people thought he was in his office.

First was about to cross the street to take a look when suddenly a light went on inside the office. The sheriff had obviously lit a lamp and that was the first time the ranger noticed how dark it was getting out. He backed into the doorway of a closed store, and the enveloping darkness actually made him feel better about what he was doing. At least no one could see him.

He was fine until somebody hissed, "Jack!" He jumped a

151

foot and his heart skipped a beat as he turned to see Clint
peering at him from the darkness.

"Come on," Clint said. "I got it."

"Jesus, I need a drink," First said as they entered the small
saloon. "I need a whiskey."

"I'll buy you one," Clint said. "Go sit down."

He got two beers and a shot of whiskey from the bartender and carried them to the table First had chosen.

"What's wrong?" he asked, as the ranger knocked back
the whiskey and followed it with a swallow of beer.

"My nerves," First said. "Watching the sheriff's office . . .
it made me nervous."

"Jack—"

"That's not what I'm supposed to be doing—"

"Listen, Jack—"

"—and I don't want to have to do it again. It's just not
right, Clint. It's not—"

Clint dropped something on the table between them and
the ranger closed his mouth.

"What's that?"

"A mask." Clint picked it up, put his hand inside and
poked his fingers out the eyeholes. "A vigilante mask."

"Where did you—did you find it . . ."

"In the sheriff's house," Clint said, dropping it on the
table again. "There's a batch of them in a bottom drawer in
his bedroom."

"Why would he need them?"

Clint stared at the younger man and said, "Same reason
he keeps extra deputy's badges in his desk at the office."

"So . . . he is the leader of the vigilantes." The ranger
picked up the mask and looked at it.

"Or he's the keeper of the masks."

First looked at him.

"Is there . . ."

"Such a thing? I don't know, Jack. I don't know that

much about vigilantes . . . but I guess somebody has to be in charge of the masks, huh?"

"Either way," First said, "we just identified one of the vigilantes."

"I call that progress," Clint said. "If I were you I'd send my boss a telegram in the morning."

"I'll do that," First said. "At first light—or as soon as the telegraph office opens."

"Put that thing away," Clint said, indicating the mask on the table. First took it and stuffed it into his pocket. "Take good care of it. It's evidence."

"Will it stand up in court?" First asked. "I mean, the way you got it?"

"Don't worry," Clint said. "I know where the others are. We can go to the house when the sheriff is there, search it and find the whole batch. Then it'll stand up in court."

First pushed the empty whiskey glass away and picked up his beer mug.

"I want to thank you, Clint, for all your help."

Clint picked up his mug and said, "My pleasure."

They both drank and put their mugs down.

"But I don't think it's over, Jack," Clint said. "We can take the sheriff in, but he may not give anybody else up."

"Then again, he might."

"We have to keep pushing."

"So they'll come after us?"

"Yes."

First patted his pocket.

"We found this piece of evidence, we can find more," First said. "Why do we need them to come after us?"

"At this point in time, Jack," Clint said, "we may not have a choice anymore."

FORTY-ONE

While Clint and Jack First were in the saloon, Roy Earl rode into town with Leo Wells and Josh Whitman. They rode right up to the sheriff's office, dismounted and walked inside.

"Sheriff Roby?" Earl asked the man behind the desk.

"That's right." Roby eyed the three men suspiciously, then realized who they must be. "Earl?"

"That's right."

"What are you doing here?" Roby demanded.

"We're checkin' in with the law," Roy Earl said. He exchanged glances with his two men. "Ain't that what men like us is supposed to do when we ride into town?"

Roby stared at the three men, saw the way they were looking at him, and realized that they didn't know who he was—didn't know his connection with Frank Waxman.

"Who are these other two?"

"Leo Wells," Earl said, pointing over one shoulder, "and Josh Whitman," pointing over the other.

"How long you boys plan on bein' in town?"

"A day, maybe two."

"Lookin' for trouble?"

Earl laughed.

"You don't know these boys, Sheriff," he said, "but you know me—you know who I am."

"I know."

"Since when did men like me have to go lookin' for trouble?" he asked.

"Well," Roby said, "just try and stay out of trouble while you're here, and we should get along fine."

"I can guarantee you one thing, Sheriff," Earl said.

"What's that?"

"If there's trouble," the gunman said, "it won't be started by us."

Roby exchanged a look with Roy Earl and he thought the man looked amused. As Earl took his men and left the office, the sheriff was having second thoughts. Did Earl know who he was? Had Waxman mentioned him to the gunman? He hadn't asked the rancher when he'd seen him earlier. He should have. Could the man have been that stupid?

Roby had always been careful about who he allied himself with over the years. He hated to think he might have made a mistake in the case of Frank Waxman.

Outside the sheriff's office Leo Wells said, "I don't much see the point in that."

"Don't you?" Earl asked.

"No."

"Me, neither," Whitman said. "We never check in with the law when we come to town."

"I just wanted to see the local law," Earl said, "check him out for myself."

"I don't think he'll be much trouble," Wells said.

"That's why you don't do the thinking, Leo," Earl said, "and I do. There's more to that man than meets the eye."

"So what are we gonna do?" Whitman asked.

"First get the horses taken care of, then get hotel rooms and then get some sleep."

"What about in the morning?" Wells asked.

"In the morning," Roy Earl announced, "is breakfast."

Wells and Whitman exchanged a glance.

"And then we do what we were hired to do?" Whitman asked.

"And then," Roy Earl said, "we'll see."

When Clint and First came out of the saloon they saw three men leading their horses away from the sheriff's office.

"Uh-oh," Clint said. "Company for the sheriff."

"Strangers just riding into town?" First asked.

"Not a good sign," Clint said, "depending on how you look at things."

"What do you mean?"

"I mean they may just be strangers passing through," Clint said, "or imported talent."

"Talent?"

"Gunmen."

"You think they're bringing in gunmen . . . for us?"

"I guess time will tell," Clint said. "Maybe the vigilantes are on the same timetable as your captain. They want this all wrapped up by tomorrow."

First looked down the street, could still see the three men. Apparently, they were taking their horses to the livery stable.

"So what do we do? Follow them?"

"No," Clint said, "not tonight."

"Then when?"

"We'll wait until tomorrow," Clint said. "Let them make the first move."

"Like shooting us in the back?"

"I don't think that's a danger, anymore," Clint said. "If these three are hired guns, they'll come at us from the front."

"Three against two," First said. "That's encouraging."

FORTY-TWO

First woke the next morning with the sun shining in his eyes from the window. This was something new. He sat up, realized he was not in his own room at the rooming house, but in Kathy Connolly's. She had invited him there the night before.

"I have a larger bed," she had said, "and we'll be on the first floor." She'd smiled and added, "Less noise, my love."

He turned his head and looked down on her. She was sleeping on her back, and the sheet had drifted down around her waist, exposing her beautiful breasts. Many things had happened to him that he had not expected—and never would have suspected—when he left Austin to come here. Perhaps the least disturbing was obtaining the assistance of Clint Adams. As far as his relationship with the Widow Connolly— if, indeed, it could be called that—he wasn't sure if that was going to turn out to be a good thing, or a bad thing.

He slipped from her bed without waking, dressed and left the room to return to his own. Luckily, he encountered none of the other roomers along the way.

In his room he washed and dressed in clean clothes. If Clint was right, and things were going to come to a head that day, he wanted to be presentable, in order to represent the Texas Rangers well—in life or death.

Clint woke that morning with Annie rolled up into a little ball and pressed against him. He reached down and stroked her naked bottom, but she didn't wake. She was sleeping very soundly, exhausted from their strenuous activities. He should have been exhausted, too, but he wasn't. If anything, he felt invigorated. Maybe it was because he knew he was going to face death that day. He'd faced it so many times before, he should have been tired of it.

He left the bed and dressed without disturbing her. As he strapped on his gunbelt he wondered how Jack First would perform when the time came. The young man's resolve to enforce the law was admirable. Today they would both find out if he had the wherewithal to do so, physically and mentally.

"You're up early," Leslie Waxman said to her husband, Frank. "Earlier than usual."

He looked up from his desk at her and smiled.

"Couldn't sleep," he said.

"Why not?"

She entered the room, her hair down, wearing her robe. She was lovely, and he wondered what he had done to deserve her. They'd met in San Francisco while he was there on business, and he had been immediately smitten. He pursued her with everything he had, and he admitted to himself that it may have been his money that finally won her over.

"Big day ahead," he said.

"Something I should know about?"

"No, my love," he said, "just business. Nothing for you to be concerned about."

She came around the desk, stood behind him and put both her hands on his shoulders.

"Is this about the ranger? And Clint Adams?" she asked.
"And the vigilantes?"

He covered her hands with his and said, "It'll all be over today."

She squeezed his shoulders and said, "I hope so." She slid her hands from beneath his and left the room.

He stood, turned and looked out the window. One way or another it would end today. He had no idea if Roy Earl would be able to kill the Gunsmith, but if he couldn't, then Adams would surely come for him, and it would end.

Sheriff Al Roby woke and dressed quickly. He didn't know when Earl and his men would try for Clint Adams and the ranger, but he wanted to be on the street when they did. Whichever side prevailed he needed to be there to see it.

When he left his house, he had no idea that anybody had been in it the day before. The bottom drawer of his dresser was still filled with extra vigilante masks.

Clint and First had agreed to meet for breakfast at the small café where Angela worked. She greeted them with a smile, but seemed to sense that neither of them wanted to talk. She brought them each a steak and egg breakfast and then left them alone.

"Did you shine that badge this morning?" Clint asked, peering at First's chest.

The younger man hesitated, then said, "Yes."

"Good."

First was surprised that Clint didn't make a joke about it. "Why?"

Clint smiled. "We'll stand with the sun behind them, and the reflection will blind them."

FORTY-THREE

Clint decided to spend the morning trying to find out where the three strangers had spent the night. Since he had no plans of his own, Ranger Jack went along with him.

"After all," he said, "we're supposed to be watching each other's back, right?"

"Never more than today," Clint said.

First they stopped at the telegraph office so Ranger First could send a progress report to his captain.

"At least this time I can report real progress," the young man said.

"Let's hope it's enough to satisfy your boss," Clint said.

After that they found the three men the first place they looked—the Laredo House, the same hotel Clint was staying in. First's badge was worth a no-argument look at the hotel register.

"Roy Earl," Clint said.

"You know him?" First asked.

"I know the name," Clint said. "He's a gun for hire."

"Is he good?"

"Supposed to be very good."

"As good as you?"

"Who knows?" Clint asked.

"You're the best there is, aren't you, Clint?"

Clint looked at the young man, then drew him to one side of the lobby.

"All I know, Jack," he said, "is that I've been better than anyone I've faced, so far. Everytime I face someone else, there's a chance they'll be better than me."

First frowned and said, "There's nobody better than you with a gun."

"Yes, there is, out there, somewhere," Clint said, "and the day will come when I meet him."

"So it could be this Roy Earl."

"Could be."

"What about the other two names?"

"Wells and Whitman," Clint repeated. "I don't know them."

"What if they're not the only three," First asked. "What if they're just the ones we happened to see?"

"That's possible, too," Clint said. "There could be some backshooters in town, somewhere—maybe to back these guys up. We're going to have to walk real carefully."

"The sheriff would know," First said. "Maybe we should ask him."

"You might be right," Clint said. "That might be better than just waiting."

"I think so."

"Or maybe," Clint said, "we should take the direct approach a bit further."

"How do you mean?"

"Come on," Clint said, "let's get out of here and talk about it."

As Clint and First left the lobby, Roy Earl and his two men came down the stairs.

"I'm starving," Leo Wells said. "Why don't we just get breakfast here?"

"Fine," Earl said. "You two go in and get a table. I'll be right there."

"Where are you going?" Whitman asked.

"Never mind," Earl said. "I said I'll be right there."

The other two men shrugged and went into the dining room while Roy Earl went to the desk. When he got there he handed the young clerk five dollars.

"Two men were just here asking to look at the register," the clerk told him, tucking the money away.

"Who were they?"

"One was wearing a Texas Rangers badge."

"And the other one?"

The clerk hesitated.

"Don't tell me you don't know who he is," Earl said, "and don't try to hold me up for more money, sonny. You won't live long enough to spend it."

"I, uh, wasn't tryin' to hold you up, Mr. Earl," the clerk stammered. "The other man was Clint Adams. Him and the ranger have been in town all week asking questions about vigilantes."

"Did they ask you about vigilantes?"

"Not this time," the man said. "This time they just wanted to look at the register."

"And did they pick out my name?"

"Yes, sir," the man said. "They caught your name right away. Mr. Adams said he knew who you was, but the ranger didn't."

"And then?"

"Then they went off in a corner and talked."

Earl gave it some thought, then said "Okay. Just keep your ears open for me."

"Sure thing, Mr. Earl," the clerk said, "sure thing."

"Oh, when were they here?" Earl asked, before he walked away.

"They was just here," the clerk said. "You just missed 'em."

Earl nodded, walked to the hotel door and looked out. He didn't see two men in the street, so he turned around and went into the dining room to have breakfast.

FORTY-FOUR

"Brace them?" Ranger Jack First asked.

Clint nodded.

"You mean . . . walk up to them and ask for trouble?"

"Exactly."

"But . . . why?"

"Because they won't be ready," Clint said. "If they're planning an ambush, it won't be in place yet."

"But if we start trouble with them, then the sheriff will have every right to—"

"The sheriff is in on this, remember?"

"That's right," First said, "but I'll still have to explain my actions when I get back to Austin—"

"If you accomplish what you're trying to do, your captain will promote you."

"You really think so?"

"No," Clint said, "but he'll thank you."

"Great."

They were standing outside the livery stable. Which they figured was a safe place to talk.

"If we brace them and make them leave—or kill them—then the sheriff and his vigilante pals will have to figure something else out. Meanwhile, we can search the sheriff's house, find the masks and you can arrest him. Maybe he'll give up some of the others."

"What if Earl and the other two are not here for us, and we force them into a fight?"

"Believe me," Clint said, "it's too much of a coincidence that Roy Earl rode into Laredo last night after dark and immediately went to see the sheriff."

"I guess you're right."

"Listen," Clint said, "are you all right to do this? Have you fired your gun at a man before?"

"I have," First said, "but I haven't killed a man, yet."

"If you want to do this a different way—"

"No, no," First said, "forcing the issue seems the right way to go. Why wait for the conditions to suit them?"

"Exactly."

"So . . . what do we do?"

"Let's check with the clerk and find out if the three men left the hotel yet. If they haven't, we can just wait outside for them."

Jack First took a deep breath. "Okay, let's do it."

The desk clerk told them that Roy Earl and his two men were in the dining room, having breakfast. Clint and First went outside to wait for them in front of the hotel.

"Just sit down and look comfortable," Clint said. There were two wooden chairs in front of the place and he pulled them over so they could sit together.

"When they come out," Clint said, "let me do the talking."

"Gladly."

"Roy Earl will do the talking for them," Clint said. "Now, don't take offense at anything I say, but make sure you know which one is Earl."

"Okay," First said. "Should I fire at him first?"

"No," Clint said, "don't fire at him at all."

"Why not?"

"Because I'll take him," Clint said. "My bet is he'll stand in the middle and the other two will fan out to both sides. You take the man on your right. You got that? Your right."

"I've got it," First said, "but you're going to take Earl and one of the others?"

"I think this is the best way," Clint said. "If you kill your man then go ahead and fire at whoever else is standing. You keep your eyes on your man and draw when he does. Don't worry about Earl, he'll try to take me first."

"And what do I do if Roy Earl kills you?" First asked.

"If that happens," Clint said, "you'll probably die."

FORTY-FIVE

Frank Waxman decided to take his buggy into town. He wanted to be there when everything went down.

Leslie Waxman waited for her husband to leave, and then she sought out Ben Pearson.

"Something's going to happen today," she told him.

"What?"

"I don't know, but Frank was up very early, and he's nervous about something."

"Like what?"

"I don't know!" she said, annoyed. "He just left to go to town. Saddle our horses. If something happens, I want to be in town to see it."

"Okay."

"And bring your gun!" she said, turning and rushing towards the house.

Pearson thought he'd bring his gun, but there was no way in hell he'd ever draw it against the Gunsmith.

Sheriff Al Roby came out of his office and saw Clint Adams and the ranger sitting in front of the hotel. He knew for a fact that Earl and his boys had stayed in the Laredo House last night, and that Clint was staying there, as well.

Clint Adams was going to force Earl's hand. He was a smart man. Why wait for everything to be Earl's way?

Roby went half a block from his office and entered the General Store, owned by Ethan Durell.

"Mornin', Al," Durell greeted.

"Ethan, you got to ride out and round up as many of the boys as possible."

"The boys?"

"You know what I mean, Ethan."

"W-what are we gonna do today?"

"Somethin's happenin' today, and if it don't go our way, we're gonna have a mess to clean up ourselves."

"Whom should I get?"

"Ethan," Roby said, "listen to what I'm sayin'. Get on your horse and round up as many of the boys as possible. Tell them to bring their hoods and their guns."

"G-guns?"

"And carry yours."

"W-who we gonna shoot?"

"With any luck," Roby said, "nobody. If our luck is bad, we're gonna have to take care of that ranger and Clint Adams ourselves."

"C-Clint Adams?" Ethan Durell's eyes popped open wide. He was fifty years old and had never fired his gun at a man. He didn't mind going along with a hanging party, but being part of a gunfight wasn't something he relished.

"Al, maybe you can get somebody el—"

"I don't have time to get somebody else, Ethan," Roby said. "You do as I say."

"Yes, yes, all right," Durell said. "Just let me tell my wife to watch the store."

"Close the damned store, Ethan!" Roby said. "Get goin'!"

Roby turned and left the store, heard Durell close and lock the door behind him. He decided to go to the hotel to have a short talk with Clint Adams and the ranger. Maybe he could put off the action until Durell came back with some of the boys.

"Look who's coming," Clint said. "Sheriff Roby."

"What's he want?" First asked.

"We're about to find out."

When Roby reached them he put one foot on the boardwalk and shoved his hat back on his head.

"Why do I get the idea you boys got trouble on your mind today?" he asked.

"Maybe," Clint said, "it's because you're smarter than you look."

"That kind of talk ain't gonna get you nowhere, Adams," Roby said.

"You know Roy Earl's in town, Sheriff."

"Do I?"

Clint nodded. "We saw him come out of your office last night."

Roby hesitated, then dug into his left ear with his pinky finger.

"Guess you got me there, Adams. That what you're doin' out here? Waitin' for Earl?"

"That's what you want, isn't it, Sheriff? Us out on the street with Earl and his boys?"

"Now why would I want that?"

"You been wanting us to leave since we got here," First said. "If Earl and his boys kill us, you get your wish. We'll be gone."

Roby looked over at the ranger.

"You ever shot a man, Ranger?" he asked.

"Not yet," First said, "but I'm looking to fix that today."

"Reckon I better have a talk with them other boys, too," Roby said. "They inside?"

"Havin' breakast," Clint said, nodding. "Why would you want to interrupt them? You'll just put them in a bad mood."

"Will I?" Roby asked. He smiled and entered the hotel.

• • •

Roby was inside for ten minutes and then came back out.

"You got them boys riled up, Sheriff?"

"I'm gonna go across to my office and sit outside, Adams. Whichever of you walks away from this thing is gonna spend some time in my jail."

"Well, I hope you feed your prisoners well."

Roby just shook his head and crossed the street. All he'd done was warn Earl that Clint and the Ranger were waiting for them outside.

"Good," Earl had said, around a mouthful of eggs, "then we won't have to go lookin' for 'em. You gonna take a hand here, Sheriff?"

"I'm just a spectator, Earl," Roby said. "I'll be watchin' to see who walks away."

"Well, we'll be out directly," Earl said. "I need me a full stomach when I kill a man."

So Roby went across the street, wondering if Earl was good enough to take the Gunsmith, or of he'd be taking a bullet in that full stomach of his.

FORTY-SIX

Somehow word got around town that something was happening, and people started to line the streets, or watch from their windows.

"What's going on?" First asked.

"My guess is either the desk clerk or the sheriff himself passed the word."

"So we're going to have an audience?"

"Not only an audience," Clint said. "My bet is some of these spectators—maybe the ones behind their windows—are vigilantes."

"So if we walk away from this gunfight . . ."

". . . we'll probably have them to deal with."

"Jesus," First said, shaking his head. "Big day."

"You scared?"

"Yes, sir."

"Good."

By the time Roy Earl and his boys stepped out of the hotel, Frank Waxman had joined the sheriff in front of his office. Leslie Waxman and Ben Pearson were part of the crowd standing in front of Little Nicky's Saloon. Nick Taylor was watching from his bedroom window. Marty Roby was also in the crowd, along with some other boys from the WX, including Gaylord Horn and Tony Dundee on crutches.

Ethan Durell had ridden to get as many of the vigilantes as he could get, but he thought Al Roby was going to be very disappointed at the reaction he got when he told those boys that Roby expected them to take up their guns against the Gunsmith.

In fact, he tried to warn Roby, approaching him in front of his office as he sat and waited with Waxman.

"Sheriff—"

"You do like I told you, Ethan?"

"I did, but—"

"Good, go stand in front of your store with your gun and wait for my signal."

"Al, I gotta tell you—"

"Whatever you got to tell me can wait," Roby said. "Now git."

Ethan Durell gave up and walked back to his store. He didn't stand on the street, though. He went inside and locked the door behind him.

"What are you going to do?" Waxman asked Roby.

"Not me, Frank," Roby said. "We. Whatever happens here we're gonna to have to clean up the mess."

Earl came out of the hotel with Wells and Whitman behind him, saw Clint and the ranger sitting there and stopped.

"You fellas have yourselves a good breakfast?" he asked.

"We did," Clint said.

"Well, let's do this, then."

Clint looked past Earl at the other two men.

"You boys got a choice, you know. You can mount up and ride out now."

The two men exchanged a glance, but it was Earl who answered for them.

"They ain't got a choice, Adams. They're gettin' paid, and they know what they got to do."

"Can't talk you out of this, Earl?"

"Hell, Adams," Earl said, "I been waitin' for you—or somebody like you—all my life."

Clint sighed. "That's what they all say, Roy."

"Come on," Earl said to his men, and they followed him into the street.

"Jack?"

"Yes, sir?"

"It's not who draws the quickest," he said, "it's who shoots the straightest."

"Yes, sir."

"And you don't have to be a stationary target," Clint said, standing up. "Move if you want. Drop into a crouch."

First stood up and faced Clint.

"Is that fair?"

"*Fair* and *dead* often mean the same thing, Jack," Clint said. "Don't worry about what's right, or what's fair. Understand?"

"Yes, sir."

"Okay," Clint said. "Let's go. And make sure you've got eyes in the back of your head."

"How do I do that?"

But Clint didn't answer. He stepped down into the street, followed by First, who moved up to walk on his right.

As Clint had predicted Roy Earl was standing in the center, and his men had fanned out on either side of him. Good help was hard to find and he doubted that the other two men were anywhere as good as Roy Earl was supposed to be with a gun. He kept his eyes on Earl, because he was going to call the play.

Clint stood his ground and Jack First put some distance between them, staying on Clint's right. Clint just hoped the ranger could shoot straight. He'd had to qualify with his handgun in order to join the rangers, so he was reasonably certain the younger man could shoot. He just hoped he didn't hesitate when it came to actually shooting at a man.

Roy Earl was not nervous. He had been through this many times before. He'd instructed both of his men to go for the ranger while he handled Adams. This was either going to be the best day of his life, or the worst, but there was no in between.

The best day of his life . . .

. . . or the last.

The town grew quiet. Clint had performed like this in front of an audience once or twice before in the old days, but not for a long time. Some bystander was likely to get hurt before this was over, but he couldn't worry about that.

He kept his eyes on Roy Earl, who stood and looked confident. He was right-handed, wore his gun low on that side. Clint knew the man would have a smooth move, as opposed to someone who wore his holster higher up. Earl's arm was dangling, and he was going to snatch his gun as he brought his arm up, and Clint would know even before Earl touched his gun just how close things were going to be and just how good Roy Earl was.

A drop of sweat dripped from Jack First's nose just before the action started, and he almost looked down to follow its path to the ground.

Almost . . .

Roy Earl's arm moved, and everything was in play. It was a good clean move, a fast move, but as Clint had told Ranger First, it wasn't who was fastest, but whose shot was true.

But he didn't have to worry about that. As Earl drew his gun, Clint knew he had him. As was usually the case for him, everything seemed to be moving in slow motion. He could see both of the other men clearly, and they were—as he had suspected—not nearly as fast as Roy Earl . . .

The gunman got his gun out and almost had it straight out in front of him when Clint's first shot struck him in the chest. A surprised look came over the man's face and his arm immediately went numb—in fact, his whole body went numb and his gun fell from his hand. It struck the ground, and then he fell on top of it.

The worst day of his life, damn . . .

Clint moved quickly and efficiently. He turned to the left and fired, and Leo Wells fell onto his back with a bullet in his heart. He had not cleared leather.

Clint looked to the right at the other man, Whitman, but he was already on his back with the ranger's bullet in his chest. He looked, instead, at Jack First, who was standing up straight next to him. The ranger had cleanly outdrew Whitman, and his first bullet struck home. But he was still standing with his gun held out in front of him, and he was breathing much too quickly.

Clint moved up alongside him and said, "Holster it. It's over."

"Is he—"

"You killed him," Clint said, "and I got the other two."

Clint quickly ejected his spent shells and fed live rounds into the cylinder.

Suddenly, First started to look around them, his eyes wide.

"What about—"

"I don't think anything's going to happen, Jack," Clint said. "I think these vigilantes draw the line at hanging an unarmed man."

"What about the sheriff?"

"Yeah," Clint said, looking over at Roby and Waxman, "what about him?"

FORTY-SEVEN

"What's happening?" Waxman asked Roby.

Roby was looking up and down the street. Nobody was firing a weapon or even had one out.

"Where are our people?" Waxman asked.

"That's what I'm wonderin'."

Ethan Durell came out of his store and made his way down to the sheriff's office while folks stood around, stunned by what they had just seen.

"Al—"

Roby turned on Durell and said, "Ethan, I thought you got the boys—"

"That's what I was trying to tell you, Sheriff," Durell said. "When I told them what you wanted them to do, about Clint Adams and all, none of them came."

Roby stared at him. "None?"

"No, none."

"Goddamn cowards," Waxman hissed. "You told me those men would do whatever you told them, Roby."

"It doesn't matter now, Frank," Roby said. "We've got to deal with Adams and the ranger now. You, me and Ethan."

"Not me, Al."

Roby looked at his number two man, Ethan Durell.

"You wanted to be a leader, Ethan. You wanted to be number two."

"For the hanging," Durell said. "That was all . . ."

"And you wanted to be the big leader," Waxman said to Roby.

Roby looked at Waxman, the rich rancher, his number one man in the Laredo Vigilantes.

"You wanted the rustler gone, Frank."

"There should have been another way—"

"Too late now," Roby said, as Clint Adams and the ranger walked over to him. "Too late."

"I'll take your gun, Sheriff," Ranger First said.

"What?"

"You're under arrest."

"Who do you think—"

"As a member of the vigilante group," First said, "and probably the leader."

"You got no proof," Roby said.

First took the mask from his pocket and showed it to Roby.

"Let's go over to your house and get the rest of these," he said, "and then I will."

Roby stared at the mask, wide-eyed.

"How did you—"

"The gun, Sheriff," Clint said. "Give it up, or use it."

Roby stared at Clint, then looked at Waxman, who had moved away, distancing himself from the sheriff.

"I'm not going down alone," Roby said.

"Al—" Waxman said, warningly.

"He was my number one man," Roby said, pointing at Waxman. And then he pointed to Ethan Durell and said, "And he was number two."

"What about the others?" First asked.

"I don't know them all," Roby said. "A lot of them came

to the meetings already masked. They didn't see us, we didn't see them . . ."

First got tired of waiting. He stepped in and removed Roby's gun from his holster, then did the same to Waxman.

"You're a fool, Roby," Waxman said. "And I'm a bigger fool for following you."

First stepped back next to Clint and looked at Durell.

"I don't have a gun," the storekeeper said, raising his hands.

"Let's all walk over to the sheriff's house and have a talk," said Texas Ranger Jack First.

FORTY-EIGHT

The next day five more Texas Rangers arrived from Austin. They assisted Jack First in rounding up as many of the vigilantes as Roby, Waxman and the storekeeper, Durell, could identify. First thought the whole thing was wrapping up too easily, but they all seemed to have the same attitude—if they were going down, everyone was.

Later that afternoon Clint was saddling Eclipse when Jack First came into the livery.

"Been looking for you," First said.

"You've got a lot to do," Clint said. "I thought I'd ride out."

"What about Annie?"

"I said my good-byes. What about you and the widow?"

"The same. Sure you don't want to help with the clean up?"

"No," Clint said, "you've got all the help you need."

First walked out with Clint as he led Eclipse outside.

"Nobody's named the foreman, Pearson, or Nick Taylor as a vigilante."

"Guess they're in the clear, then. Looks like maybe they

were just being used by Mrs. Waxman, who's probably after her husband's money."

"Maybe she'll get it, now," First said.

"Maybe," Clint said, "and those two will end up with nothing—like the sheriff. He thought helpin' Waxman get rid of the rustlers was somehow going to make him rich."

Jack First put his hand out.

"I don't know how to thank you," he said. "Without you I'd be dead."

"You're going to do fine, Jack," Clint said, accepting the man's hand. "You're a fine Texas Ranger."

"For a man with no sense of humor, right?" First asked, smiling.

"I don't know, Jack," Clint said. "Was that a joke?"

Watch for

THE BIG FORK GAME

270th novel in the exciting GUNSMITH series from
Jove.

Coming in June!

J. R. ROBERTS

THE GUNSMITH